# AN INDEPENDENT SPIRIT

Janet leaves home to take up a scholarship to study equitation under Baron Von Bleiken, a retired dressage champion. At the Centre, Janet is surrounded by new faces. Phillippe, the Baron's grandson, immediately seems attractive, but Janet feels challenged by him over her riding skills. Max Thornton is a quiet, thoughtful man who seems more than interested in Janet. As the Centre prepares for a major competition, conflicts and passions lying beneath the surface emerge . . .

ANGELA DRACUP

# AN
# INDEPENDENT
# SPIRIT

*Complete and Unabridged*

**LINFORD**
*Leicester*

First published in Great Britain in 1984 by
Robert Hale Limited
London

First Linford Edition
published 2002
by arrangement with
Robert Hale Limited
London

British Library CIP Data

Dracup, Angela
An independent spirit.—Large print ed.—
Linford romance library
1. Love stories
2. Large type books
I. Title
823.9'14 [F]

ISBN 0–7089–9816–X

Published by
F. A. Thorpe (Publishing)
Anstey, Leicestershire

Set by Words & Graphics Ltd.
Anstey, Leicestershire
Printed and bound in Great Britain by
T. J. International Ltd., Padstow, Cornwall

This book is printed on acid-free paper

To my family — with love

# 1

If Harold Anderson had not come on the scene things might all have turned out very differently. Janet would certainly not have taken up the offer to study dressage under the supervision of the famous Baron von Bleiken, she would not have met Phillippe Géraudin — never have been introduced to Alexa Firth's wealthy brother Max.

But Harold Anderson had come along at the beginning of a crucial year of decision-making when Janet was suddenly faced with opportunities she would never have thought possible. During the course of that year he had, as the saying goes, swept Janet's mother off her feet. The wedding was planned for the end of June, just before Janet's course was due to commence.

My dear, sweet, dizzy, romantic mother, Janet thought as she attempted to smooth her newly washed hair into some sort of submission before pinning one of the five dozen red roses Harold had sent her mother to the lapel of her new cream crêpe de Chine shirt.

Her mother, in the next room, was in a flurry of dressing, packing, scent splashing and violent emotions.

'Janet,' she wailed, appearing tragically in the doorway, 'do you really think this dress is all right?' Janet tried not to show amusement as she regarded the oyster-pink silk dress which had cost her mother a fortune and which she had taken out of tissue paper nightly for the last six weeks in fond anticipation of this great day on which she would wear it.

'Yes,' Janet was patient, 'it's lovely — really lovely.'

'You don't think I should wear the mint-green?' her mother went on with persistence.

'Mother dear,' Janet said with solemn firmness, feeling as she so often did that her mother was really the child, not she,

2

'your mint-green is perfect for going away in. The one you have on is just right for getting married in. You look wonderful and you shouldn't change a thing!'

Her mother's eyes filled with tears. 'Oh pet, you're always so good and sensible. I do hope you're going to be all right without me,' she finished somewhat illogically.

'Of course I will.' Janet tried to keep a light note — any slight revelation of her occasional anxieties about the changes that were about to take place in her life would be disastrous for her mother to share in. Mrs Holt, soon to be Mrs Anderson, was a copious weeper. Once she started it took a long time to stop. If she began to cry she would never reach the church on time — besides which her make-up would be ruined.

'I wish you weren't going to be so far away,' her mother mused.

Janet smiled, they'd been through it all before. 'It's only 100 miles — hardly the other side of the world!' she said gently. She put her arm around her mother. 'I'm looking forward to it,' she reassured her, 'even more so now that I know you're going to be happy and well looked after.'

Her mother's cheek flushed like a girl's. She sighed. 'Yes' — she said breathily, 'I'm so lucky.'

A car drew up outside. Her uncle, Stephen Holt, had come to collect them. Janet ran downstairs to greet him, leaving her mother to make final adjustments to her appearance.

'Is your mother anywhere near ready?' he asked, giving Janet an uncle-like kiss.

'Somewhere near,' Janet said with a little grin and a small wink.

He allowed his features to relax into a slight smile. He was just as she remembered her father, his brother — stern, solid, uncompromising, utterly trustworthy and with a heart of gold. He had helped them so much since her father died four years ago. They could not have managed without him.

'I hope people don't think it's funny,' he said gruffly, 'this giving your mother away business.'

'Of course they won't,' she said. 'You know mother is determined to have all the traditions at this wedding; she must be given away by a male relative — and you're the chosen one!'

'I'm the only one daft enough to agree,' he said in his blunt Yorkshire way. Then, 'What are you doing?' he said in alarm as she advanced on him with a fern-garnished carnation — thoughtfully provided by the future groom.

'Making you look the part,' she told him, arranging it to nestle against the navy cloth.

'Oh Lord!' he groaned. He looked at his watch and shuffled in agitation. 'Come on, Mary,' he said under his breath, 'we're going to be late.'

'Don't worry,' Janet said, hearing her mother's footsteps on the stairs, 'it's all going to be fine.' She felt a sudden rush

5

of optimism, not just that the wedding would go smoothly but that things were really going to get better for her mother. The years of widowhood had been dreadful. Mrs Holt had been so helpless, so lost. Janet felt that Harry was going to be perfect for her; offering protection, security and a tendency for romantic sentimentality her mother would bask in. It wouldn't do for me at all she thought, but mother will love it.

As the three of them stepped outside the front door, Mrs Holt gave a little shriek.

'Good Lord,' Stephen said, 'whatever's the matter?'

'I haven't got a handkerchief,' she breathed.

'Well go back and get one,' he hissed fiercely. He stood in grim silence on the step. Then suddenly he laid a hand on Janet's shoulder. His voice had a low tenderness she could not recall hearing before.

'I'm glad you're going to do some living for yourself, love,' he said. 'It's about time. Even the toughest towers of strength need a break now and then.'

His words came back to her later in the quietness of the church as her mother stood at the altar steps. She felt enormously grateful for Stephen's recognition of her responsibilities over the last few years, for certainly she had had to draw heavily on inner psychological resources to provide her mother with the practical and emotional support she needed. A feeling of intense excitement and apprehensive exhilaration bubbled up inside her at the thought of the opportunities and challenges ahead, so that it was an effort to maintain an appropriately solemn expression on her face. And marriage was a very solemn thing, she thought, as she listened to Harry's calm voice giving assurances that he would love and honour her mother until death did them part. She prayed that things would go well for them. She felt they were well suited — Harry a respectable widower of 50 with a grown-up family, a secure job, an easy-going temperament — and her mother, just a little younger, with a great desire to cherish and be cherished, with no other ambition than to be a good wife, a loving mother and a comfort-providing homemaker.

The vows were coming to a conclusion. 'And all my worldly goods with thee I share,' Harry was saying. 'In the name of the Father . . . '

The words drifted away into the coolness of the church as Janet reflected on this material aspect of her mother's new relationship. Harry had already set about sharing his worldly goods — in fact he had been quite shamelessly indulgent. Flowers, jewellery, chocolates — all the traditional romantic gifts had been given in abundance. Janet had not been left out either, but for her the gifts had been more practical — perhaps reflecting his view of her as a very different person from her mother. There was a beautiful pen, a leather-bound diary — and books. Books relating to her 'A'-level studies in

English and French — and, of course, books on horsemanship, stable management and dressage.

Harry was not a wealthy man but his job as head of a small local comprehensive provided a secure and steady income which was riches compared with what Janet and her mother had had to manage on in the last few years. Janet had left school at sixteen in order to provide some income for herself and her mother. Mrs Holt had been proud of her daughter's assumption of responsibility, yet worried that she had missed the opportunity of furthering her education. Working at the reception desk of a local hotel and helping out in the dining room did not seem to offer many prospects.

And now when their luck had changed Janet appeared determined not to retrieve what Mrs Holt felt had been lost. She had gone so far as to enrol for 'A' levels, studying at the local Further Education College in the evenings, but she had not been prepared to commit herself to any further academic study.

'Such a shame for you not to finish your education, dear,' her mother had said as they sat with Harry over Sunday lunch some weeks before. 'Properly I mean — university and so on,' she added vaguely.

'Mary,' Harry said, in his gently pompous way, 'education is not solely about going to university. It's about broadening experience and developing skill, learning to be self-reliant, managing relationships and so forth.'

'Mmm,' Mrs Holt was impressed yet doubtful, 'but it won't *get* her anywhere will it, not like training to be a nurse or a teacher. I mean it's just jumping about on horses — I thought girls grew out of that.' She glanced at Janet's face and was immediately full of remorse. 'I'm sorry,' she said, patting her hand, 'I just don't want you to be nothing, like me.'

'Well, dear,' Harry said gallantly, 'if you hadn't been a trained secretary and come to do a bit of typing in our school office things might have been very different.'

And yet, Janet reflected, as she moved up the aisle following Harry and his bride into the vestry, her mother really did not want her to have a career at all. Nothing would please her more than for Janet to marry a young doctor or solicitor, settle down and have a family.

But that's not for me, Janet thought. I'm going to do something on my own account. And as her mother stood with her new husband on the church steps, happy once more under a loving man's protection, the spirit of independence that had struggled and fluttered in Janet's breast, almost without hope in recent years, trembled to be set free, to take wing and soar away unfettered into the waiting world beyond.

# 2

Independence on bus, train and foot, however, was not nearly so glorious a thing when one had a case to carry and the early July rain spilled down in grey ribbons, stinging the eyes and tracing cold rivulets down the back of the neck. The taxi driver had been very firm about not driving his car up the half-mile mud track which led to the famous stables situated in the calm greenness of a North Yorkshire valley.

'Sorry, luv,' he had said, 'but I've had bad times here and when you've argued with a horse box once — you don't risk it again.'

Janet understood his feelings and set out purposefully through the mud. She had hoped to look neat and smart for her meeting with the Baron von Bleiken who was to give her an hour of his precious time to initiate her into the studies and work schedule she was to follow for the next six months. Her heart sank as her feet did into the mud as she felt the brown wetness springing up her calves. Her hair curled into dripping snakes around her face and she could taste traces of make-up as she licked the drips that ran over her nose and cheeks.

Half-way up the lane she became aware of the guttural roar of a car's engine. She flattened herself into the hedge as the noise became more insistent. There was the sudden panic-stricken fear of physical injury as the car sliced past her in a cold rush of air. It was braking fast, the bonnet tipping exaggeratedly forward as the tyres somehow gripped the mud and the car came to a halt. The passenger door was flung open and a man's voice drawled lazily, 'Allow me to make amends.' He made a delicately courteous gesture of invitation, indicating that she should get in the car beside him. She hesitated, uncertainty and a feeling of helpless foolishness at her dishevelled appearance holding her back.

'I don't bite,' he said. 'Come on, get in, I'm getting wet.' He stretched over, took her case and hauled it onto the back seat. She could sense his gaze on her as she folded herself into the car and wiped her face with the back of her hand.

'You're lucky,' he said, grinning.

She was puzzled. 'I'm sorry?' she said questioningly.

'Lucky that you can manage to look great when you're half-drowned and covered in mud,' he said, still grinning.

'Oh!' she said lamely, wishing she could think of a clever reply.

'Do you make a habit of wandering about in downpours heaving a suitcase about?' he asked drily.

She felt a little stung by the question. She was desperately tired after her journey, apprehensive in the strange surroundings — in no state for holding her own with a handsome young man driving a fast sports car. And he certainly was handsome; black hair, olive skin, sharply defined features, and that was only the beginning. She turned away, afraid that he would think she was gawping if he should take his eyes from the rain-drenched lane ahead.

'The taxi driver went on strike at the bottom of the lane,' she told him, feeling a great sense of relief that she was not presenting herself as a tongue-tied, bedraggled nobody.

He raised his eyebrows — splendid dark glossy brows — in approval. 'He tipped you out, did he — I hope you didn't tip him in return?'

She laughed. Relaxation began to thaw her cold limbs a little.

'Are you coming to join us?' he asked. 'A new recruit to the slaughter?'

She wondered if she detected a trace of sarcasm in his voice, but he was still smiling. She decided that he just liked to make his questions sound funny and amusing. He must be a member of staff at the stables, she thought. She wondered if she would be seeing much of him?

'Well,' she said, more lightly than she felt, 'I hope it's not going to be as bad as that.'

'Terrible life here,' he said cheerfully. 'Up at six, work and slave all day, go to bed with no more damage than screaming muscles if you're lucky. Four months ago I took a broken collar bone with me but I'm as good as new now.'

'Oh dear!' she murmured politely, well aware of the risks riding involved.

He certainly looked in peak condition now, exuding the kind of pent-up energy one associated with a crouching panther. His skin was wonderfully brown, taut and polished like a gleaming new conker. He could not have got a tan like that in the English summer, surely.

She felt a little sorry when the car stopped. She doubted if she would see much more of its driver on her own. She imagined a girl, tall and slender-limbed with a mass of black curls and violet eyes sitting with him in this fabulous car. She suddenly felt like a mole-coloured little nobody and frowned slightly because it was not a feeling she had experienced before.

He was regarding her, his eyes narrowed and glinting under silky black lashes. 'Don't worry,' he said, 'I didn't mean to put you off — you'll get on fine here. My grandfather will love you.'

He uncurled himself suddenly from the car, swinging her case over the seat in one easy, graceful movement. 'I think he's expecting you,' he continued as he came around to open the car door for her. 'Go through the white door there and take the second on your right.' He gestured towards an arched wooden door set centrally in a beautiful stone house which faced them across a walled-in, cobbled courtyard.

She swallowed hard, anxiety suddenly pushing aside all other feelings. 'Am I late,' she asked, glancing shyly up at him, 'for my interview. It was for three o'clock.'

'One minute to go,' he said, looking at his watch.

'Oh,' she murmured faintly.

He smiled. 'I'll take care of the case,' he said. 'Good luck!'

How kind he was, she thought, to rescue her in her hour of need. She had never been rescued before by such an indisputably beautiful man, for she could see now as he strode away that his figure was equally as impressive as his face. Lean muscular hips and legs were shown to advantage in tastefully faded jeans and there was a slender strength about his shoulders currently concealed under a sage-green bomber jacket. He was quite splendid. She remembered that he had mentioned his grandfather, but had not volunteered any information as to who he was. She was intrigued and angry with herself for not having had the initiative to ask him outright.

She continued to watch as he walked away. Without turning back he raised his hand in a casual gesture of farewell.

She flushed, realising that he must have had some awareness of her interested appraisal.

Janet, she told herself sternly, pull yourself together. You came to this place for a serious purpose. You saved up for a year to come and you're going to do well; not be put off by the first proverbial pretty face you come across.

As she entered the house she had to keep swallowing hard as anxiety set her salivary glands working overtime. She smoothed her hair with a shaking hand and tried not to think about her mud-splashed legs.

The house was still and silent. Its main door led into an oak-panelled hallway with a central staircase leading up to the first floor. The furnishings were sparse, well-worn and classical. The polished wood block floor lay gleaming and uncovered apart from one small silky rug centrally placed. A large oak chest and a grandfather clock faced each other from the corners of the room, standing out starkly against the plain white walls. The clock had a comforting fat tick with a steady, unperturbable rhythm. It soothed Janet's agitation by giving three ripe chimes as she knocked on the door at the end of the hallway. Knocking produced no effect, although faint sounds could be heard beyond the door — the rustling of paper perhaps. With firm resolve she opened the door and looked inside.

It was an airy room with deep casement windows and chintzy curtains. There were papers, magazines and charts on every possible surface. A bookcase filled with books ranging from massive leather-bound volumes to slim paperbacks took up the whole of one wall and the other three were covered with paintings, pastel drawings and pencil sketches of horses and dogs. A fire burned welcomingly in an open grate surrounded by a carved stone fireplace.

The occupant of the room stood with

his back to Janet, engrossed in the papers on the desk. She cleared her throat and shut the door gently to attract his attention. He turned to look at her, a man of medium height and build with a sweep of silver hair falling across his forehead. She judged him to be around seventy. His face was not unduly lined but had a look of serenity about it which she rarely noted in a younger man.

On seeing her his features lit up. He made an urgent beckoning movement with his hand. 'Come and look at this, my dear,' he said. He had turned back to the papers before she joined him at the desk and was running his fingers down the columns drawn neatly on the page.

'It's a food chart,' he explained. 'I work on this each day before tea time.'

She looked with interest and noticed that each column was headed in beautiful italic capitals with a horse's name. What lovely names they had, she thought, smiling — Rum Baba, White

Opal, Roving Rainbow, Yorkshire Pudding, Smiling Princess and Con Brio. Her heart leapt as she read the last two names. They were almost household words, names of champions who could go on to international fame in the future.

'I list all the staple feed they consume here, how much they're wanting and how it matches against their performance during exercise — look,' he went on, indicating some figures sketched in red ink, 'I rate them on each movement daily, using a five-point scale. I can tell straight away if the diet isn't suiting them.'

Janet was startled. She knew that a horse's diet affected his level of energy and skill of performance but she had always considered this an incidental factor. Surely the famous Baron did not put more stress on a horse's feeding routine than on his breeding or the skill of his rider.

'I'm glad you don't say anything, my dear,' he told her. 'These things need thinking about before one judges.' He started at the paper, obviously engrossed in his own thoughts and barely aware of Janet's presence.

'This is the really important thing,' he said, pointing to a starred item marked 'delicacies' which appeared at the base of each column. 'This is the key, to find out what gives them real pleasure, what they regard as — how shall I put it — a personal luxury.'

He pushed the hair from his eyes impatiently. 'People think for horses, carrots and apples or mints will do.' He looked at her fiercely. 'Never apples, my dear, never, they give a horse terrible wind, awful pains. Carrots, possibly — but these are so boring. These horses are kings and queens — one does not feed them on a humble vegetable like some donkey. One has to find out what their oysters are, if you follow my meaning.'

'Now Opal, he loves green peppers — just a little chopped small each day after exercise. And Baba, he likes nuts — ' he held up a warning finger, 'only walnuts — not any nuts. Princess,' he exclaimed fondly — 'she adores champagne — I'm afraid we cheat a little on weekdays — we give her non-vintage sparkling burgundy — but on Sundays,' he turned to glance mischievously at her, 'it's the real thing!'

Janet moistened her lips. She felt she was getting out of her depth and the Baron had not really acknowledged her as a person at all yet.

He straightened up and looked directly at her. 'Pleasure and kindness, my dear. That is what makes a good horse superb.' He reflected, 'You see, we have taken away much of their being, stolen their spirit to use for ourselves. We keep our good horses shut up in a little box and deny them the freedom to run and fight in the herd, or gorge themselves on rich spring grass. We do all that in order that they do marvellous and clever things to bring us fame, prestige and money. So it follows, in return we give them the subtlest of kindness and individual consideration we can. Don't you agree?' he finished with faint challenge, obviously wanting a reply now.

She nodded slowly. 'Yes,' she said softly, 'I think I understand what you mean.'

'We all go better for kindness and that precious little spark of individual consideration, do we not?' he queried.

'Oh, yes!' she replied, at last able to agree wholeheartedly.

'It's simple, is it not?' he said.

She smiled. 'Yes — of course.'

He gave her a critical appraisal. 'You're not very big, my dear.' What could she say? There was no denying her lack of inches. 'Five-foot two?' he suggested. 'Seven stone.'

She laughed, amazed at his accuracy.

He was serious again. 'It doesn't matter,' he said, 'you have good proportions for riding, longish legs and arms despite your small stature. And a horse wants to know about your soul more than your legs — some riders have no soul, however long their legs and strong their back muscles. Your legs will do quite well,' he concluded abruptly. She smiled inwardly, recalling her anxiety about the splashes of mud. How trivial that worry seemed now — how utterly irrelevant to the judgement and philosophy of Baron von Bleiken.

He fell quiet, pensive again. The rattle of cups could be heard on the wood floor outside.

His face shone with pleasure. 'Three-fifteen,' he said, glancing at a brass-framed wall clock near the fireplace. 'Time for tea.' The door opened and a rather grim lady pushed in a trolley laden with delicious-looking food.

The Baron thanked her graciously and held the door open as she left the room.

'My housekeeper,' he said. 'She came to work for me many years ago.

Janet thought that he must inspire

loyalty to keep a member of staff so long.

'Now,' he said with huge anticipation, 'we shall enjoy ourselves. I hope you have a good appetite.' He motioned Janet to sit down.

'Will you pour please, my dear?' he asked, leaning back and stretching his legs towards the fire. He closed his eyes in obvious contentment, giving her the opportunity to observe him. He was an interesting figure in his full-coated woollen jacket, breeches and hairy socks. His hands, relaxed on the arms of the chair, were old hands thickly piped with purple veins and his face was heavily traced with lines indicating the progress of the silent finger of time. He had an aristocratic air about him but no hint of inconsiderate arrogance — more the faint eccentricity of firmly held, highly personalised convictions.

The silver tea-pot was heavy and Janet found herself having to concentrate hard on her task of pouring.

What a strange interview this was

turning out to be. She wondered if the Baron knew who she was or if he was simply happy to talk to anyone who provided a captive audience. He had not mentioned her name once or given any indication of knowing why she had come. And yet the references to her size and its relationships to riding skill gave a little hope that the interview was not going to be totally futile.

'Please help yourself,' he said, giving the impression that he expected her to eat a lot. The contents of the trolley were mouth watering; hot floury scones melting with butter, tiny open sandwiches, buttered fruited tea-cake, shortbread fingers, glazed triangles of pastry glistening with white icing and cherries and a magnificent chocolate cake on a filigree silver cake stand. But Janet was not able to respond positively to the quantity and splendour of the food as sensations of hunger were currently overlaid with natural feelings of hesitance and insecurity in these new surroundings. Yet she was concerned not to offend her host by rejecting his hospitality.

She chose a sandwich and a scone and tried to make them last.

The Baron applied himself to the food with vigour.

'You have good hands, my dear,' he observed, pausing from his eating when some minutes had passed.

She looked down at them. They were smallish and squarish with short unvarnished nails. She had always thought them unremarkable.

'Kind hands,' he said, 'peaceful — not always fluttering about like a startled bird.'

'Oh,' she said limply. It was difficult to think of a fuller reply. There was another silence while he ate.

He looked at her speculatively. 'My dear girl,' he said slowly, 'I am an old man.' He smiled into the fire. 'I am also a rich old man, and so I can afford to try and make some of my dreams come true.'

She looked questioningly at him.

'That is what this scholarship you have won is — a dream I have had for many years but have only recently been able to put into practice.'

She leaned forward with eager interest.

'I wanted to give young riders of proven ability, integrity and determination a chance to have the best instruction available and also the chance to ride some of the very best horses — for they can, perhaps, teach you more than the greatest of human instructors. Horsemanship — whatever anyone else tells you to the contrary — tends to be a rich man's pastime.' He shrugged — 'Oh you can get a promising young horse cheap but he may never come to anything and the rest are beyond the reach of most people. I have horses out there worth thousands of pounds and then you have to feed them and pay for the vet when they are sick.' He spread his hands out with feeling. 'A young lady like you could never own and keep a really good animal.'

'No,' she said, warming to him, 'that's right.'

'Of course!' he agreed.

'I liked your application,' he said, 'it was simple and honest. You wanted exactly those opportunities I have mentioned. You were not asking for the moon. I always check with the applicant's instructor. Your Mrs Laycock indicated that you were a young woman of some determination. I gather you worked as a waitress in order to earn money to pay for instruction at her stables.'

'Yes,' she said, with a feeling of grateful affection for the blunt, tough woman who had taught her all she knew about riding and horses.

'So,' he said, 'we give you a lot of chances and we teach you as best we can and at the end of the six months — who knows?' He shrugged expressively, 'May be nothing will come of it all — but you will have learned — education in its widest sense.'

Echoes of Harry's words came back to Janet as he spoke, lifting the corners of her mouth in a slight smile.

The Baron had completed his tea. The trolley was almost empty.

'One final thing, my dear. Although you are not here to learn to be a teacher, I always ask my scholarship students to take on one or two pupils for I think that attempting to teach someone else an art is one of the best ways to teach yourself. I have arranged some sessions each week — of course, you will be paid,' he added as an afterthought.

Janet nodded — she already knew of these arrangements which had been carefully set out and explained in the literature detailing the terms of the scholarship. She would not have taken up the option to come to the stables had she not been able to be self-supporting.

He seemed to be dozing off. Janet wondered if she should leave, but as yet he had not given her any specific information. She was at a loss as to what she was supposed to do next — where she should go.

'Er — do you have a timetable for me?' she asked a little nervously.

There was a considerable pause. He appeared perplexed.

'Ah' — he suddenly remembered, 'Phillippe has all the details.' His eyes closed again, he seemed to have dismissed her. She sighed inwardly and got up to go. She had reached the door when he spoke again. 'My dear,' he said sleepily, 'Phillippe is my grandson. He is still young.' It was as though he were making a statement of condemnation and a plea for tolerance at the same time.

'But he is a good rider. One day he may be great.' He tilted his head back and crossed his arms over his chest. It was clear that their conversation was finally at an end.

Janet shut the door quietly behind her, then stood for a moment pondering on the interview. She felt exhilarated yet strangely disturbed by what she had heard. She did not understand just what the Baron expected of her and could she fulfil those hopes even if she were to grasp the precise nature of them? His words had been uplifting but frighteningly vague.

She decided to find Phillippe in order to get some concrete instructions. She had that sudden feeling of helplessness that comes from being in an unknown place where one has no idea of the little routines and procedures that help to make one feel at ease and wanted. She did not even know where her case and her belongings were. She gave herself a shake of assertion and strolled out of the house with an outward confidence belying her inner emotions.

The courtyard was quite deserted. She looked around, trying in vain to find some clue as to where she should go next.

A voice came from somewhere above her head.

'Miss Holt,' it said, in a lazy, yet unmistakably commanding drawl. She detected the source of sound instantly. It came from the top of a stone flight of steps leading up from the courtyard to an unlikely looking door which must at one time have been a large high window in the old coach house block. The figure on the steps was even more handsome than she remembered. So this was Phillippe — the Baron's grandson — her gallant rescuer from the rain. Her heart gave a small leap which she chose to ignore.

'Come up here into the office,' he said, 'and I'll fill you in on what you're supposed to be doing.'

He led the way to a small, neat, business-like room furnished with a desk, chairs and several filing cabinets. At his invitation she settled herself in a chair facing an attractive arched window. He sat on the edge of the desk swinging one of his long slender legs gently to and fro. There was a short silence during which she felt acutely aware of his renewed appraisal of her. She hoped he would not ask for any comments on her meeting with the Baron. She did not feel prepared yet to voice any judgments.

'Well!' he said briskly — 'we let you off any further ordeals for today — give you time to settle in and have a leisurely look around. I'm afraid we've had a slight problem with accommodation,' he continued, frowning a little. 'There was some fire damage recently to one of the flats the scholarship students live in so we've arranged for you to share with someone,' he hesitated for a fraction of a second, 'Miss Smythe-Pollock.'

'Oh, I'm sure it will be all right,' Janet assured him hurriedly, very keen to fit in with any arrangements which he thought suitable.

'Good,' he said approvingly.

He picked up some papers from the desk and tapped them with his long brown fingers.

'Your timetable,' he said. 'I hope it's self-explanatory but if there's anything you want to query, don't hesitate to come and see me.' His tone had suddenly become almost curt. He was drumming his fingers on his thigh, tapping his foot restlesly as though he could not wait to be off and away somewhere. She felt curiously deflated.

'I'll show you where the flat is,' he told her, jumping off the desk and motioning to her to follow as he moved to stand by the window.

She could see as she looked down on the courtyard that the house where she had seen the Baron formed the centre of a three-sided stone building. Phillippe explained that the house had once been flanked by a coach house and stable block. They were currently standing in the latter — now converted into flatlets and offices.

'You will be living over there — in what used to be the stables,' he said, pointing to the building opposite. 'It has been — as they say in the brochures — tastefully modernised!' He looked down at her with a wry smile; she was very conscious of his nearness, his powerful lithe masculinity and the brilliant blueness of his eyes. To her annoyance she felt the blood rising in her cheeks, pinkening her face like that of an excited little girl.

He turned away suddenly: 'Right,' he said, 'that's it then.' He looked at his watch. He was restless again, pent up like some caged jungle cat.

'Yes — ' she said with forced cheeriness — 'well — I'll go and settle in.' She ran lightly down the steps and across the courtyard. She wondered if he was watching her and wished she had the confidence to give him the casual kind of wave he had given her earlier on.

# 3

Lavinia Smythe-Pollock was stretched out on the sofa in the sitting room of the flat she and Janet were to share; surrounded by magazines, fruit, a bag of nuts and several bottles of nail varnish.

Janet's entrance produced a smile of delight on her face.

'Oh Lord,' she said with fervour, 'am I glad to see you — I'm so bored I could die.' She patted a small clearing on the surface of the sofa. 'Come and sit here and tell me all about yourself,' she said invitingly. 'Can't shake hands, pet, I'm still tacky,' she went on, displaying elegant pearly pink nails. Her smile was wide and warm, from a pair of full rounded lips surrounding a magnificent set of white teeth. There were auburn curls falling in masses down to her shoulders, eyes like golden syrup and the sort of classically-shaped nose that needed no improvement. She was as beautiful as Phillippe was handsome. Janet could not remember seeing so much physical magnificence in one day.

'I'm Lavinia,' she said helpfully. 'Most people shorten it — it's the most dreadful mouthful. I do prefer Vinnie — Lav just doesn't conjure up the most pleasant images.' She sat back and stared openly at Janet. 'Darling,' she said with some concern, 'you look absolutely clapped out; go and lie down immediately.'

'Oh, but I'm fine,' Janet said, feeling a little like a daisy in confrontation with an orchid.

'But you must be fit for tonight!'

'Tonight?' Janet said questioningly.

'Yes,' her companion said, as though surprised Janet was not already prepared for whatever was in store. 'It's my birthday and Daddy's given me a blank cheque to spend on a dinner for all my friends in this godforsaken place!'

'Oh!' Janet did not wish to be ungrateful but she felt that by 9 o'clock she would be ready to fall into bed rather than set out on birthday revels.

'Eight o'clock — ' Vinnie said. 'At the Thornlea — it's absolutely *heavenly*, the food is simply out of this world.' She patted her shapely figure. 'I simply *adore* eating!'

Her voice had a rich creamy texture about it and she spoke with dramatic emphasis, the words rising and falling like waves on a beach.

She looked quizzically at Janet. 'Have you been to see the Baron?' she asked.

Janet nodded.

'I hope you didn't eat enough of his tea to spoil my dinner!' she complained. 'I must have put on half a stone the last time I had tea with him,' she added reflectively.

'Are you starting your course this week, like me?' Janet asked her.

'Oh heavens, pet, no, they don't run two poor hacks in harness at once!'

'Oh dear,' said Janet, making an

exaggerated pretence of an alarm she was beginning to feel, 'is it as bad as that?'

'It's jolly hard work here,' Vinnie said with feeling. 'I never want to get up at 5.30 a.m. again as long as I live.'

'Aren't you going to take up a career in riding then?' Janet asked innocently.

'Oh, my Lord!' she exploded, closing her golden eyes in horror, 'never in a million years. I'm not a student like you, pet, just a vague friend of the family; I've been helping out with schooling one or two of the horses for a few months — just filling in time.'

'Goodness!' Janet said, marvelling at the way Vinnie could adopt such a casual attitude to such an important job.

'I'm just hanging on here until I get married,' she explained.

Even in the gloom of that dull afternoon Janet could see the ring on Vinnie's left hand trembling with a fiery white brilliance.

'Umm,' said Vinnie, slipping her arms

gracefully over her head and wriggling her hips into the sofa cushions, 'Peter J. S. Villiers is the lucky man. He's already incredibly rich and he's going to be terribly famous.'

Janet felt a little shocked at this open boasting, but Vinnie was so warm and open it was impossible not to like her.

'Have you got a lovely man tucked away somewhere?' Vinnie asked, a wry smile tilting the corner of her lips.

Janet considered. It sounded dull to say no, but there really wasn't anybody. She had had a boy friend a year ago but he had taken a job in another part of the country and they had lost touch.

'No one at present!' she said cheerily.

'Good girl,' Vinnie said with approval, 'it's good to be independent. I wish I could be,' she sighed and ruffled her hair. Janet didn't believe a word of it.

'It's positively desperate here on a Monday,' Vinnie complained. 'It's our day of rest. The weekends are absolutely chaotic, with clients coming to school their horses and dressage competitions and so on. You can't move an inch for horseflesh and trailers. We're all absolutely dead by Sunday evening. So Monday is decreed by the Baron to be preciously guarded for the relaxing of body and spirit. No one is allowed to do a thing. The horses get fed and then they languish in their little boxes — and we, alas, do the same! Oh, my God,' she said, 'sometimes I don't think I can bear it a moment longer.'

'Do you know the Baron well?' Janet asked cautiously.

'Well actually, darling, he's a distant uncle. I've known him since I was a teeny little girl. He's an absolute pet — not nearly so nutty as some people make out. But he has got a trifle more eccentric recently.'

Janet wondered who the people were who scorned the Baron's ideas and thought him 'nutty'.

'Actually,' Vinnie said thoughtfully — 'he talks a lot of sense does the old darling — and he's fearfully loyal and generous if he takes a liking to you.'

It was obvious that the Baron had taken a liking to Vinnie. Janet longed to ask about Phillippe but decided to wait. Vinnie was bound to comment sooner or later and Janet preferred not to give any indication of an interest in Phillippe.

Later on, the question of what to wear for Lavinia's birthday celebrations perplexed Janet as she soaked herself in the small pine-walled bathroom. It seemed that the occasion was going to be a grand one demanding something special. She would have felt most comfortable in a shirt and slacks but thought that possibly the rather formal navy dress with the big white ruffly collar which her mother had bought for her would be more suitable.

She wondered, as she brushed her hair and applied some shadow to her eyes, who would be included in Vinnie's party at the Thornlea restaurant. Apparently Peter J. S. Villiers was in Europe on business and therefore not able to join in the festivities. She thought of Phillippe — his lean brown frame and finely-chiselled features — would he be included in the party? Her heart gave another leap and she pursed her lips fiercely — resisting the temptation to apply more scent, she arranged her hair in a sleek seductive curtain over one eye.

She waited until the last minute before slipping the dress on.

The silky material with its taffeta lining slithered easily over her hips but the zip fastener did not seem inclined to make such smooth progress. She tugged uselessly at it, knowing that she was only making matters worse.

Vinnie was both skilful and sympathetic when appealed to for help. 'The wonders of modern scientific inventions!' she commented, teasing the soft fabric out of the little nylon teeth. 'Still I suppose it must have been a most dreadful bore with all those tiny buttons and loops they used to have. There — I've done it,' she exclaimed at last, 'but I'm afraid you've suffered slight damage, darling — you'll have to be careful when you're taking it off or you'll get stuck again.' They were casually spoken words but Janet was to recall them later in rather different circumstances.

Vinnie herself was totally stunning in pale green satin pyjamas decorated with gauzy silver butterflies. Her auburn hair was tantalisingly caught up with two glittery silver hoops and her eyes with their lids delicately shaded in metallic green shone like a rare liqueur brandy.

'You look super!' she said to Janet, then she tilted her head on one side as though slightly puzzled. 'I've got it!' she declared and dashed into her bedroom. Janet could see through the door that the room was a tangled jumble of clothes, shoes and make-up. How anyone could emerge from it as elegantly groomed as Vinnie was a miracle.

'Here,' said Vinnie, 'put these on — they'll make you look positively edible with that deliciously demure dress.' She was referring to a string of pearls which Janet suspected were real and which Vinnie was already clasping around her neck.

'Oh, I don't think I should wear them,' she said nervously.

'Why not, they're absolutely perfect?' Vinnie explained.

Janet had to agree, she was amazed and delighted at the way the tender paleness of the pearls turned the skin of her neck and throat to a rich creaminess she had not noticed before.

'Good,' Vinnie said, showing herself as a lady not to be argued with, 'that's settled then.'

A bright blue Range-Rover drew up outside with loud insistent hoots. Vinnie shrieked with delight and ran out to greet the passengers. The two men in front she kissed with an enthusiasm which made Janet wonder what Peter J. S. Villiers would have thought. However, Vinnie's greeting of the girl in the back seat was equally ardent so perhaps he would not have minded after all.

She hung back, feeling an over-whelming shyness and trying to take some comfort from the sharp smells of the countryside, the earthy dampness rising up from the cobbles, the rain-washed blue streaks showing brightly between the broken clouds promising a fine evening with an hour or so.

'Janet!' Vinnie called commandingly. 'Come on!'

The three girls sat together in the back seat. Janet was introduced to Poppy, then Mark and Robert. Their relaxed, friendly manner made her feel instantly welcome and she sup-pressed the lurch of disappointment at Phillippe's absence.

The Thornlea restaurant stood at the end of a curving drive surrounded by smooth lawns and massed beds of shrubs and flowers. It was an elderly house with a welcoming, comfortable look about it. Creepers and pink roses entwined together on the mellow Yorkshire stone walls and a cosy glow of peach-coloured light came from the large mullioned windows. The garden had an informal air about it, the lawns being obviously cared for but not closely clipped and trimmed, the surrounding flowers being allowed to range in bright profusion.

Vinnie and her party poured out of the Range-Rover, a gay, sparkling, laughing bunch. Janet was sure that no one would fail to notice their arrival; her companions seemed to be making enough noise for twice their number. She recalled going to restaurants with her mother and Harry on one or two occasions. They would stand soberly and correctly in the reception area assimilating the atmosphere and adjusting their behaviour accordingly. Her companions tonight showed none of this accommodating attitude. They burst in on the restaurant as though about to take it by storm, determined that everyone should share in their exuberance.

A man in a dark grey suit came down

the hallway, a calm smile on his face. As he approached the noisy, laughing group Vinnie advanced to meet him and flung her arms around his neck.

'Max, darling!' she cooed, 'it's absolutely years since I've seen you!'

'Yes,' he said drily, 'it must be at least two weeks.'

He was smiling at her in a kindly rather uncle-like way. He did not, however, return her embrace, neither did he incline his head towards her and he was tall enough to be out of even Vinnie's reach so there was no chance of her giving or getting a kiss. She disentangled herself undismayed. 'It's my birthday,' she told him, 'and we're all going to have a wonderful time and spend absolutely heaps of money, so you'll make lots of lovely profit and be even richer than you are now!'

'Good,' he said, his eyes twinkling with wry amusement.

'You know everyone, don't you?' Vinnie said, her continuous flow of chatter like an ever-gurgling mountain stream.

'Ah!' she said mysteriously as his eyes turned towards Janet. 'This is Janet; she's only just arrived and she's most dreadfully quiet and shy and I simply don't know what we're going to do with her!'

Janet bit her lip. She felt Vinnie had gone too far, drawing attention to her unnecessarily, making her appear even more gauche than she was beginning to feel in these new surroundings.

The big man looked thoughtfully at her. He offered his hand. 'Hello, Janet,' he said in a simple, direct way, 'I'm Max Thornton.'

Janet's irritation suddenly vanished under the firm pressure of his handshake and the quiet authority in his voice.

She smiled up at him.

'This is a beautiful house,' she said, glancing down the hallway at the wide curving staircase and the elaborately moulded plasterwork surmounting the doorways.

He paused, making serious consideration of her remark.

'Thank you,' he said gravely. 'I would like to show it to you when things are not so busy.'

He sounded as though he meant what he said. He smiled, excused himself and walked away towards the dining room.

Vinnie was temporarily a trifle subdued. She squeezed Janet's arm. 'I think you've made a hit there, pet!' she said mischievously.

Janet laughed, pleased to find her usual self-confidence restored. 'Do you know him well?' she asked.

Vinnie gave a mock shudder of pleasure. 'I only wish I did!' she breathed huskily. 'He's divine,' she went on, 'a positively heavenly host!' She gurgled appreciatively at her own wit.

Before Janet could reply she noticed the black, sleekly curved bonnet of a Porsche turn into the drive.

Phillippe's car! A jet of excitement sprang up inside her. She tried to recall Vinnie's last remark, but it and the big man with the gentle brown eyes who was its inspiration, receded into the background with Phillippe's arrival.

He strode in with the easy enviable confidence of the indisputably handsome and talented. He was wearing close-fitting cream-coloured slacks and an open-necked shirt in a soft shade of milky coffee — most effective in maximising the impact of his supple, muscular figure and his fantastic tan. He moved towards them, his eyes flickering over the group and as they came to rest on Janet he gave a brilliant smile as though she were the one person in the world he wanted to see. Happiness surged through her and she could feel the tremble in her cheek muscles as she smiled back.

A faint shadow crossed Vinnie's face as he kissed her coolly and correctly on her cheek.

'I'd almost given you up,' she

murmured. Janet wondered if she was angry with him. He certainly did not get the usual overwhelming Vinnie-style greeting.

'What's all this?' he asked energetically, 'a birthday and not drinking yet to celebrate?' He held his hand up commandingly. A waitress appeared as if by magic.

'Two bottles of Cordon Rouge '76,' he told her. 'We'll have it straight away — I presume you have some suitably chilled?' He was stern almost to the point of intimidation.

'Oh yes, sir!' the girl assured him anxiously. He smiled. The girl gaped at him in open admiration. 'I'll bring it straight away!' she said.

The champagne was indeed cool. It misted up the tall shiny glasses as soon as it was poured. Phillippe took a long drink. 'It'll do,' he told the girl slowly — 'in fact it will do very well!' She received another smile and went away looking more than happy.

'Breaking hearts again, poppet?'

Vinnie enquired almost maliciously as she studied the menu.

'Not at all,' Phillippe said calmly — 'it's a simple question of demanding good service and value for money in a way that ensures you get it.' He shot a swift glance at Janet. 'Isn't that so?' he asked.

'Yes,' she said, disciplining her voice severely so that it sounded firm and certain. 'But I think I should need a little practice,' she added. 'I don't think I could do as well as you yet.' She was surprised at herself for making this observation. She drank some more champagne; it was really delicious. Phillippe looked at her with amused interest.

'Why ever not?' he asked.

'Well,' she shrugged, 'people wouldn't take so much notice of me!' She could hardly say that people took notice of him because he was devastatingly handsome and assured, because he was poised and significant, because he was attractive and sexy and male. Not even the effect of the champagne would give her the courage to be so frank and open.

'You may be proved wrong one day,' he said softly, giving her a hard piercing look. 'You look the sort of girl people would take a lot of notice of.'

Her mouth went dry, sweat prickled under her armpits. She gave up any attempt to tell herself that she had not been deeply affected by meeting him and that being in his presence was pleasurable almost to the point of pain. It was incredible to think that just a few hours ago she had not even known of his existence.

They all sat down to eat.

The menu was short and unpretentious. In some ways it hardly did justice to the food that subsequently arrived. After a day with very little to eat Janet was suddenly ravenously hungry and full of anticipation of a splendid meal. She was not disappointed. She chose home-made iced watercress soup served with warmed buttery garlic bread and fresh cream. Then there was grilled chicken and tarragon with an accompaniment of crisply cooked vegetables and salad. The champagne was flowing freely. Phillippe commanded more bottles to be brought.

Vinnie, sat on Phillippe's left, seemed to have abandoned the rather cool manner she had shown to him previously. She was chatting to him now with lively animation and he listened half-attentively — occasionally glancing lazily towards Janet. His blue eyes had darkened in the softly lit room to a deep glowing brilliance and his tanned cheeks had taken on an almost silvery sheen. She could see the lean hard lines of his chest through the thin stuff of his shirt. Her heart began to quicken as she watched his long restless fingers drumming on the table. She imagined the touch of his hands on her skin and a dark thrill of previously unknown desire shot through her body. Mark was speaking, questioning her politely. She could barely concentrate sufficiently to give him proper answers.

She noticed Max Thornton standing in the doorway of the room — quietly scrutinising the occupants. His calm gaze rested briefly on her and he smiled his gentle smile. Her feverish excitement subsided a little, she felt vaguely troubled. She tried to smile back but her features were strangely out of control. She took another gulp of champagne and redoubled her efforts with Mark.

She decided on the raspberry mousse to finish. Phillippe declared himself tired of champagne and ordered two bottles of claret and fresh glasses. The mousse and claret arrived together. They were both superb but Janet was now past the point where she could appreciate them. Her limbs felt curiously light and her hands seemed clumsy and disobedient as she manipulated the cutlery. There were some slightly burnt-tasting almond biscuits to go with the mousse. They were temptingly arranged on a silver tray which the waitress placed in the centre of the table. Janet reached for a second, having been pleasantly puzzled by the unfamiliar taste of the first.

She could never clearly recall what happened in the few seconds before she became sharply aware of the spilled wine flooding over her dress — the empty glass lurching across the table and falling to the floor — the upturned plate of mousse nestling in her lap. She was drenched in humiliation. A few moments of helpless suspense passed whilst she glanced around her. No one seemed to have noticed. Vinnie and Phillippe were deep in conversation. Richard and Poppy were holding hands on the table and Mark was totally absorbed in a pot of crême brûlée.

Her hands quivered uncontrollably as she righted the plate and slipped it back on the table together with as much mousse as she could scoop up. She pushed her chair back and tried to stand. The room shivered before her as her legs struggled to cope with the task of supporting her body. For a moment she was terrified that she might topple over — that everyone would know she had drunk too much champagne . . . and then there was a firm hand under her elbow guiding her towards the door, supporting her unobtrusively so that she was able to make a steadier exit than she would ever have thought possible.

She was pulled through a door at the back of the hall and half-carried up a flight of narrow steps which led to a softly carpeted landing. The noise of the restaurant receded into the distance, making Janet aware of the loud singing in her ears.

★   ★   ★

Max Thornton was a practical man, used to coping with the little emergencies his customers provided. He did not, however, usually carry them off to his private flat and personally dust them down. But in this case his sympathy had been aroused by the pale, slender girl struggling to hold her own at a giddy birthday party in an alien environment.

'Don't worry,' he reassured her, 'everything will be all right.'

Her dress was soaked at the front. It would need sponging and drying. He guided her through the bedroom into his own personal bathroom.

'Slip the dress off,' he said, 'and I'll have it back to you in no time, as good as new.' The kitchen staff would do a quick mopping job and the tumbler drier only took a few minutes. He handed her one of his bathrobes and tactfully left her alone to change.

Janet was now in a state of bewilderment. She was dimly aware of being in a beautifully furnished, warm bathroom; of mellow golden spotlights, leafy plants, glittering dolphin-headed taps on a round azure-blue bath, and beyond in the bedroom the soft blueness of walls and carpet lit solely by two milky full moons above the bed.

With enormous resolve she got up from the stool he had placed her on and raised her arms to reach for the top of her zip fastener. The sharp movement left her giddy and breathless. Tiny pink globules of light swam in front of her eyes. She made herself stand straight and managed to move the zip down about four inches. It stuck — fast. She began to tug at it, dimly remembering a similar problem earlier on. The pink globules surged in abundance and the muscles in her arms quivered with fatigue. She sat down again, a feeling of hopeless panic seizing her.

Someone was coming up the steps. It must be Max Thornton returning for her dress; she was past caring, although for a fleeting second the thought that Phillippe might find her in this state speared her with a fresh shaft of desperation.

Max looked solemnly at her. 'Oh!' he commented, in his dry way.

'My zip's stuck,' she said pathetically, daring to face up to her helpless state by looking him in the eye.

He tilted his head a little and his mouth twitched at the corners.

'Right then,' he said briskly, 'we'll have to sort it out.' Without hesitation he put his hands under her armpits and lifted her to her feet. 'Can you stand?' he asked, turning her around and applying himself to the zip without delay. She nodded in dumb misery.

'I feel so ashamed,' she moaned suddenly. 'I don't usually behave like this.'

'I'm sure you don't,' he said cheerfully.

Then, 'What do you think of my champagne?' he asked conversationally as though they were just having a little chat, whereas in fact he was about to unzip her from her dress and underneath she was wearing no more than a bra and the briefest of painties.

'I drank too much,' she said tragically.

'He laughed. 'You liked it then!' He seemed to be making some progress with the zip, his hands were very sure and certain; she began to stand up with more confidence, the pink globules had gone and the dizziness was not so overwhelming.

'I import it specially,' he went on. 'It means going to France a lot which is not an unpleasant way to pass the time.'

'Oh, it sounds marvellous,' she told him. 'I've only been abroad once — on a school trip.'

'I bet they didn't take you into a wine cave, did they?' he asked.

'No,' she giggled, 'nothing like that.'

'Strictly museums and art galleries?' he suggested.

She was on the point of telling him all about it, he was so relaxed and easy to talk to, but the dress was undone now and he was slipping it down over her hips. Before she had time to be conscious of her nakedness he had placed the bathrobe around her shoulders. He turned her towards him, wrapping the edges of the robe together and knotting the belt. It was all done quite coolly in a considerate yet disinterested way.

'There!' he said, looking questioningly into her face. 'Feeling better?' he asked gently. The sympathy in his brown eyes unsettled her. It made her think of home and her mother. They seemed so distant. The events of the day glided before her — a jumbled medley of sounds and images: the rain, the Baron's unpredictable remarks, Vinnie's exuberance, the black Porsche, sharply chiselled features in a tanned face. Phillippe! Whatever would he think of her now?

She bit her lip. Tears of wretchedness and exhaustion were pushing in her throat. Her companion continued to watch her. 'Do you want to cry?' he asked in his courteous, business-like voice. He was standing close to her, his tall solid bulk filling her field of vision. For a fleeting moment she thought how good it would be to rest against him, to abandon herself to a bout of self-pitying sobs. She sensed that to lay her head on that broad chest would be comforting and uncomplicated, with no questions asked, no obligations incurred.

But she was not a girl to cry easily. She swallowed hard and squeezed out a smile. 'No,' she said faintly. He grinned.

'Five minutes then,' he said, laying her dress over his arm.

She sat on the bed. Delicate music was drifting from the room across the landing. It had a troubling sweetness about it. She shivered slightly inside the thin robe. Her cheeks burned but her body was icy cold. She felt dull and heavy as though she could hardly move. He came back soon, gave her a concerned, appraising look, then dressed and zipped her up with the same detached efficiency with which he had undressed her.

'Oh dear, I don't know what you must think of me,' she said miserably.

'I think you're a very tired young woman trying to cope with strange people in new surroundings who isn't used to a lot of champagne,' he said gravely.

He was very reassuring, better than an uncle — she always felt a little awkward with them.

He was smiling, about to say something.

But he said nothing and gave a gentle sigh.

'Do I look all right?' she asked weakly.

'Almost as good as new!' he said.

He took her arm and escorted her to the stairs. She was much steadier now but still numb and stiff. She felt completely at ease with him, and alarmed at having to face the birthday party again.

As though to give her back her dignity he suddenly became quite formal. 'I do hope you enjoyed some of your meal,' he remarked.

'Oh, yes,' she said, wishing that her stomach would not reel at the mention of food. 'It was lovely.'

'You never got round to the mousse

did you?' he enquired.

'Those little biscuits!' she said sadly. 'I only had one!' She did not know whether she was glad or sorry — they had certainly been her undoing.

'Ah, the amaretti' — he told her, 'little Italian macaroons; they're becoming quite difficult to get hold of.'

He was still talking to her as they returned to the restaurant. It was almost deserted now. The table they had sat at was empty.

Phillippe was standing by the window smoking a cigar — looking cool and composed.

He raised his eyebrows quizzically at the sight of Janet.

His smile was faintly mocking.

'The wanderer returns!' he remarked. 'Come on, I'll take you home.' He moved briskly towards the door. Max continued to hold her arm until they stepped into the clear air of the garden where the roses slept underneath a gauze-shrouded moon.

'Good night,' he said gently. 'I think

you'll be all right now.'

Sitting beside Phillippe in the Porsche it seemed like a hundred years since she had sat there before.

'Thank you for waiting for me,' she said. 'I'm afraid I've been a nuisance.'

'The Baron would never forgive me for abandoning one of his little protégées,' he said. 'And I would never forgive myself,' he murmured, turning briefly towards her. She felt a slight return of giddiness, perhaps not entirely brought about by the champagne she had drunk earlier.

# 4

It was disturbing, next morning to find that the evening's events presented themselves with sharp clarity for review and inspection.

Janet tried hard to ignore the pictures that kept switching on in her head like a series of holiday slides.

'Are you all right, darling?' Vinnie enquired from the other side of *Vogue* and a wedge of toast lavishly garnished with butter and honey.

Janet declined to admit that her head was filled with an insistent rhythmic thumping, her body as fragile as the shell of an egg.

'Fine, thanks,' she said, eyeing the contents of the breakfast table with a shudder.

Vinnie poured some coffee, strong and black.

'Drink this,' she said, 'and don't eat a

thing until lunchtime. There could be a disaster. You're supposed to be riding in half an hour, sweetheart.'

'I know,' Janet said. She had looked at her timetable some time in the middle of the night when she had woken full of remorse, anxiety and homesickness. It was a heavy schedule: riding, study, the day-to-day care of three horses and an hour's teaching at 4.30.

She drank the coffee. 'Oh,' she groaned, 'I feel terrible.'

'You look it, darling,' said Vinnie, 'but you're bound to be O.K. You strong northern girls always are.' She stretched luxuriously, casually beautiful in a blue velvet house robe.

'Yes,' Janet agreed stoically, 'I'll be O.K.'

'I'm madly jealous,' said Vinnie. 'You seemed to get to grips with Max Thornton without even lifting a finger. He never takes the faintest notice of me.'

Janet could not resist a smile; it hurt

the inside of her head terribly.

'What do you mean?' she asked.

'Well, he seemed quite taken with you,' Vinnie said — 'and he's so gorgeous.' She tilted her head in consideration — 'There are many dishes at the Thornlea,' she gurgled, 'but he is quite definitely the best, something of a local delicacy.'

'Well, he was very kind,' Janet agreed, 'but he was just being helpful, that's all!'

'Ah, well,' Vinnie sighed, pouring herself more coffee, 'they do say that he's a teeny bit fussy about his women. Many are called but few are chosen and so on,' she added vaguely.

Janet wondered why she was so interested. She also wondered what effect it would have had on Vinnie if she had told her how she had stood in Max Thornton's bathroom while he undressed her down to her bra and pants! What a night it had been, she thought.

Phillippe had been very kind too. He

had driven her right up to the door and waited in the car until she found her key before roaring away over the cobbles.

She dressed carefully before going out. Spotless navy stretch jodhpurs, a check cotton shirt, shiny black boots and a navy velvet hat did a lot to restore her self-confidence as she looked in the mirror. And yet today somehow she wished she were a little taller, that her hair was a more definite colour, her eyes more startling than the clear grey that looked back from the mirror.

Stepping out of the house she was instantly aware that the stable yard was full of life. Horses were being fed and groomed and their loose boxes raked out, wheelbarrows trundled along delivering and collecting. Their contents wobbled vigorously, spilling over onto the concreted area between rows of boxes. A team of brushes and rakes darted about clearing up debris as fast as it fell. It was all so familiar. Wherever there were stabled horses the scene at around 8 o'clock in the morning never changed. Janet immediately felt part of the scene — any awkwardness at the sight of so many strangers melted away like a snow shower in April.

She walked along the rows of boxes looking for the horses she was to care for. She consulted the names on the sheet Phillippe had given her; September Morning, Pepperpot and Little Nell. The labels on each door gave the occupants' name, year of birth, gender and height. So it was not difficult to trace the animals she wanted.

She found Pepperpot first — 'Pepperpot 1975, gelding 15.2 hands', said the little white card on his box, neat and correct like a visiting card. He turned out to be a beautiful grey, evenly flecked with dark brown speckles. His eyes looked impassively at her but she knew from the energetic flickering of his ears that he was alert, intensely aware of the presence of a new person. She opened the door and slipped into the box, murmuring softly as she ran her hands along his head and neck, letting him know he could rely on her protection. She started on her task of grooming him with satisfaction. People passed by, smiled, said 'good morning', accepting the presence of a new person without comment.

September Morning was a bright chestnut with startling orange eyelashes. He was a little restless under strange hands but presented no real problems. It was 9 o'clock before Janet got round to Little Nell; who turned out to be a sizeable bay mare with a nicely defined white star on her forehead.

She had almost completed her work when she became aware of a man's figure standing outside the box. 'Good morning!' an unmistakable voice said briskly. Phillippe, immaculate in jodhpurs and sweat shirt, was generating a degree of impatient tension which caused Janet to catch her breath. There was a quivering pent-up energy in him that was almost visible. 'Come on!' he said, 'it's time you'd finished with all this nonsense. I want to see you ride, not waste your time like this.'

'That's a little unfair,' Janet said evenly. 'It was down on my timetable to feed and groom these horses before my ride.'

'Yes,' he brushed his hair swiftly from his forehead, 'I know! Get September tacked up and bring him into the teaching area as soon as you can.'

Janet moved fast and within minutes was mounted on the chestnut, trotting him gently round the covered school where most of the instruction at the stables took place.

It was a large area carpeted with shredded bark, enclosed by roughly planked walls and surmounted by a high arched roof. Sounds from both inside and out were muffled, giving the feeling of a small enclosed world all on its own.

Phillippe stood in the centre of the school whilst Janet and September circled around him. He gave sharp barely audible instructions to let her know when he wanted to see a change of pace or a turn. Janet soon settled to September's trot, so smooth and fluid that she felt as though she was sitting on wheels rather than legs. She began to enjoy herself.

Phillippe did not share her satisfaction. He called her to a halt, his expression full of a harsh concentration amounting to severity.

'You're suffering from last night's over-indulgence!' he said coolly. 'Your style is nice but the horse is hardly moving, he's almost asleep.' His words fell around her like stinging slaps. A tidal wave of disappointment engulfed her. Not to have a horse 'going forward' was one of the most basic criticisms that could be applied to an aspiring rider.

Phillippe vaulted on the horse, moved him into a trot, then stung him sharply with his whip. September threw up his head and lashed out with his hind legs, swivelling them around sharply and hitting the planked wall. A splinter shot into the air. She could see Phillippe mouthing something through his teeth but his body remained relaxed so that the horse after his initial protest settled readily into an active springing trot. Janet was full of admiration; she could see that the horse's energy had doubled, yet he remained beautifully balanced, fully in control.

Phillippe turned and smiled — the dazzling, brilliant smile he had given in the restaurant. It was like turning on a spotlight. There was an open intimacy in that glowing gesture.

'There you are!' he said, as he circled past her. 'It's easy.'

Once remounted, Janet could tell immediately that Phillippe had woken the horse up, sharpened his awareness, increased his keenness to please. He leapt forward with eagerness, his cornflake-coloured mane rocking vigorously.

The heavy wooden door swung open and the Baron walked in. He stood in silent watchfulness. Janet sensed that for all his gentle manner he had the eyes of a hawk.

'Don't let me disturb you, my dear,' he called. 'Just go along as you are.'

It was not easy — to be sitting on a strange horse watched by two experts whose eyes seemed to be boring into her, catching each little adjustment of movement, noting any tiny deviation from their notion of the ideal riding style.

After a while the Baron called her to a halt. He stood for a few moments appraising her and the horse in silence. Phillippe remained a few yards away, his face curiously blank and disinterested.

'Yes,' the Baron said slowly after a while. He began to nod his head in rhythmic thoughtfulness. 'Yes,' he repeated. 'It is not at all bad.' The slight trace of European accent in his voice was more marked than Janet had noticed the day before. He touched the horse's mouth. A light coating of greeny foam glistened on his finger as he held it up for Janet's inspection.

'This is good,' he said. 'He's salivating, he's wanting to do his best for you, he's really listening.' He smiled at her. She saw that he was wearing his woollen jersey inside out and back to front. The label stuck up arrogantly against his throat. His eyes followed her glance, noted the quick suppression of a smile. 'Ah,' he said, tugging at the jersey, 'I'm old; I can afford to be a little — how do you put it — crackers!'

She felt somewhat ashamed.

'Don't worry, my dear!' he reassured her, 'these things don't matter, not at all. Now,' he said with importance, 'I want to see you again — this time asking the horse for a lengthening of stride in his trot. I want to see a beautiful curve here in his neck, and the quarters nicely balanced — no swinging about!'

The two men watched in silence as their pupil drove all her powers of concentration into the task in hand. It was a simple enough exercise — yet deceptive in simplicity. To achieve a good extension of a horse's legs at trotting pace demands subtlety on the part of both horse and rider.

September was going well but Janet felt that he was not making full use of his capabilities. The trot was brisk and swinging rather than long and flowing; he was not really reaching out at all. She knew what Phillippe's remedy would be — a shortening of the reins and a hard, elongated squeeze with her lower legs. Somehow she sensed that the Baron would not be in sympathy with such tactics. Indecision and frustration gripped her. The horse, absorbing the tension of his rider, suddenly broke into a little preliminary buck before freeing himself into the easy pace of a gentle canter.

The Baron called her into the middle again. He shook his head in kindly resignation. 'You try too hard, my dear, too hard.' He curved his arms into a gesture of supplication as a conductor might do in an attempt to urge the most tender notes from his orchestra. 'There is no pleasure, you see,' he gazed reproachfully at her. 'No pleasure for you — nor for him either.' He fondled the chestnut's ears, creasing his face in thought. 'You must not *tell* him — my dear — he is a great horse — a true gentleman.'

His face was heavy with concentration, with the effort of conveying to her how he felt. 'You must *ask* him — ask so he cannot refuse and then you help him with the way you feel, how you adjust your muscles. You do it all with your head — you think of his stride lengthening — long and beautiful — and it will happen.' He tapped his head and whispered — 'It's all up here.'

He sent her out into the arena to try again. It was then she noticed that Phillippe had gone. The previous conflicts were lifted from her and suddenly she felt the horse reaching out underneath her, his legs extending into the longest, most fluid trot she had ever experienced. Round they went, completely at one with each other, fully united in their striving for the delicate perfection the Baron sought.

He began to give gentle commands, asking for changes of pace and direction, walk, trot, canter, small circles and loops, and gradually the requests became more complex — exercises she had only briefly attempted before. Everything seemed to fall into place, the horse was ready to do all she asked — as though there were some close secret between them — the true oneness of horse and rider. Her mouth curved into a smile of contentment, happiness flowed through her body and limbs.

The Baron looked thoughtful as he called her to a halt. He ran his hand over September's glossy, tightly muscled neck and looked at horse and rider in solemn contemplation. Janet was getting used to these long pauses in the Baron's words and actions. She realised that there was no cause for uneasiness. It was just his style.

'That was most interesting,' he said slowly. 'You have authority — my dear — and yet you are kind, most sensitive, very unusual in one so young.' His voice had dropped to a murmur as his head sank down towards his chest. He stood there in silence as though in a dream. Seconds passed.

Phillippe returned leading a delicate-legged bay horse with wary, anxious dark eyes. The horse stood in agitated submission whilst Phillippe tightened the girth and ran the stirrups down. He sprang onto his back and moved away, flicking a glance towards Janet as he passed her. There was a sharpness in his eyes which she had now come to expect as though he were seeing into the depths of her. It was excitingly unnerving.

'Grandfather,' Phillippe called patiently, as though calling someone from sleep, 'I've brought Brio for you.'

The Baron's head jerked up. His face was alight with interest and affection.

'Ah, Brio!' he murmured. 'Now we shall see something beautiful.'

And indeed they did!

Both horse and rider were beautiful in their own right but moving together they blended into a fluid gracefulness and purity of movement which touched the emotions like watching the swaying outline of wind-blown trees carved across an evening sky.

They gave a display of technical perfection which Janet had never seen equalled.

There was the quietness of the walking pace, with Brio peaceful and receptive, his limbs moving in flawless symmetry. And then the brilliance of the trot — lengthening into the famous 'passage' when Brio elevated his legs without in any way decreasing the length of his stride. They came cantering in a diagonal line across the arena, Brio as collected and precise as a precision dancer. Just before the centre point Phillippe brought him back to a trot — she could hear the Baron counting the hoofbeats: '1, 2, 3, 4,' then they were away again into the canter, circling round in perfect balance.

Phillippe glanced towards his grandfather — a question in his eyes which the older man interpreted instantly.

'Yes,' he said, nodding, 'yes — I think so.'

He turned to meet Janet's puzzled gaze. 'He's going to try the piaffer, my dear. We haven't quite got it right yet, we must keep trying.' He gestured to her to dismount from September and move him away from the centre of the arena.

Janet watched in silent suspense. The piaffer movement was notoriously difficult, demanding the utmost in control, balance and obedience from the horse. Only the most skilled and experienced rider could bring the horse to that point where he was able momentarily to suspend the great mass of his heavy muscled body in an elegant and lofty trotting gait in one spot.

Phillippe circled Brio around and

once more achieved the fluid elongated passage. The exquisitely timed hesitation in Brio's trot filled Janet with a great tenderness for the animal, that he should be prepared to make such an effort solely for the pleasure of human beings. They reached the centre point, slowed down, ceased going forward. She could see the concentration stretching the skin across Phillippe's features like wire strings. She held her breath. There was almost a moment of triumph and then Brio's head slumped. The light went from his eyes. He stood — leaden and dejected, all movement seemingly drained out of his body.

Phillippe let out a click of exasperation. 'Let's try again,' he said, ignoring his grandfather's faint protest.

They tried again — twice more — but it was no use. The horse was upset, the harmony had gone.

'My poor Brio,' the Baron said, 'I don't know how to make him happy.'

Phillippe prepared to dismount. The Baron was looking at Janet, apparently absorbed by her hands.

'I wonder,' he said, 'if you might be the one to talk to my Brio so he understands.' He spoke very softly. Phillippe was absorbed in feeling over Brio's legs, checking for any evidence of unsoundness. She hoped quite desperately that he had not heard. She was flattered by the Baron's remarks but well aware that only one expert rider should handle a horse the calibre of Brio. And that there should be any suggestion of her skill being equal — leg alone surpassing — that of Phillippe's, would be unthinkable.

Phillippe would have every right to be furious at such an intimation.

His expression, however, was cheerful as he turned to his companions. 'Ah, well,' he said, with a shrug, 'another day, perhaps.'

The Baron smiled. He slipped an arm around his grandson and then to Janet's surprise drew her towards him with the other. 'You young people must go and enjoy yourselves in this beautiful countryside,' he said. 'Take these two horses out through the fields and make them think that life is worth living.' He released them both.

'I shall go for my coffee,' he announced abruptly, and without further comment he left them.

Phillippe grinned. 'Ten-thirty,' he said. 'Time for coffee and the odd slice of black forest cake!'

Janet smiled, thinking of the Baron's afternoon tea the day before. 'That was a very impressive performance,' she said shyly.

'Thanks,' he said. 'Well, it looks as though we have to go out for a hack. Grandfather's orders are not to be taken lightly.'

She glanced at him curiously. It was so hard to know when he was serious.

'Take time off for coffee first,' he said decisively. 'I'll meet you in half an hour.' They walked together down the arena, leading the two horses.

'And take September's tack off,' Phillippe said lightly — 'He's had enough for this morning — there's another horse I want you to ride instead.

The substitute for September turned out to be a black gelding of truly majestic proportions.

'We call him Little Chief,' Phillippe said sardonically. 'He's a 4-year-old — no more than a baby in my grandfather's eyes.'

Janet looked up at the horse. He must be fully 17 hands, she thought. Some baby!

'I'll give you a leg up,' Phillippe said in his lazy casual drawl. She bent her leg at the knee and he placed his hands on her shin bone.

'Now!' he said, indicating that she should spring up. He supported her with the deftness of a dancer lifting his prima ballerina so that she landed in the saddle as lightly as a bird. Her skin tingled where he had touched her.

They walked out together, following a continuation of the track which led up to the stables. Beyond the stables the fields spread themselves under the blue hills in the distance. The track curved around the field's edge and ended abruptly in front of a high, barred gate.

Phillippe nudged Brio towards the gate and bent down to release the chain which fastened it. As the gate swung open he beckoned Janet through with a flourishing gesture.

'Madam!' he said, smiling. His brilliant eyes pierced her again, sending a wild surge of happiness through her nerves.

She pressed her legs on Little Chief, feeling a slight resistance in the horse's massive quarters. But there were no real problems, he moved majestically through. From then on it was magic — riding out with Phillippe through the waving grass, the sun overhead turning from a silver thread behind the clouds to a golden ball. Pockets of golden sunshine nestled in grassy hollows and the remains of the previous day's rain glinted like shining mirrors.

They walked in silence for a while.

'We'll open them up a little in the next field,' he said eventually. 'It's too tough here for these cosseted animals. Brio's never seen a cross-country course in his life!'

'What about Chief?' she asked.

'Oh, he's a lot to learn,' Phillippe said non-committedly.

She longed to ask him things — about his family, his friends, his ambitions. Silly things like his favourite colours and preferred foods. And, of course, whether there was a girl somewhere; someone very precious and cherished.

He said, 'What do you think of my grandfather's ideas on horsemanship?'

'Interesting,' she said carefully.

'Yes.' He swivelled his eyes towards her. 'Certainly interesting. I've never managed to make a horse go by thought transference though — have you?'

'Not quite,' she admitted. 'Did he teach you?' she added with interest.

'Yes — among others.' He lapsed into

silence, his face suddenly closed up, his thoughts inaccessible.

When they got to the next field Phillippe warned her to keep a tight hold on Chief before they set off into a canter. He urged Brio forward and the horse responded with a great squeal of joy. Janet knew that Chief was just as excited. His great black neck rocked in front of her, his mane flying out wild and free. She shifted her weight onto the stirrups and raised herself slightly out of the saddle, bridging her reins over the horse's neck. It was like riding the wind, she thought, giving herself up completely to the joy of blending into the power of a living animal.

They slowed down to a trot. Phillippe turned to look at her, 'O.K.?' he said.

'Very, very O.K.,' she told him breathlessly. He narrowed his eyes slightly. She had a swift sensation of having being over-exuberant, over-familiar. He was warning her not to go too far.

They walked on for a few minutes,

then halted. Straight ahead was a decaying mansion built of golden Yorkshire stone weathered and mellowed by the seasons. It showed all the signs of years of abandonment. The roof sagged, the windows without glass or draperies were as doleful as dead eyes. Tufts of grass sprouted through the stonework, and creepers twined long fingers over the rotting main door.

'Cobweb Palace,' Phillippe said drily. 'It used to be Greenfern Hall. The Green family went bust in the 1930s and vanished abroad. Nobody claimed the house — except the wildlife.'

'It must have been splendid,' Janet said.

'Yes — we can walk along the terrace, it makes interesting viewing — you can see right in.'

The horses' hoofs clattered alarmingly on the stone terrace, seeming to shatter the peace of the dead house. Janet felt rather like a trespasser.

And then it happened; it was only to be expected really. A party of rooks disturbed from the shelter of the house retaliated by sailing into the soft afternoon air in a flurry of furious screeching. The flapping wings cut a path straight in front of the horses and Brio shied in terror, cantering away to the end of the terrace. Chief stood for a brief moment, as though anchored to the ground. Suddenly his great head was flung up — that movement in itself almost unseating Janet — and she prepared herself for a swift bolt. But what happened was far worse. He began to plunge — throwing his neck down and then twisting around, swinging his quarters first one way and then the other. The rolling sideways thrust destroyed any efforts to maintain balance, yet still she remained on his back. His movements began to change and now she could feel power pulsing down his length. She knew that if he threw his legs out to the back she stood little chance of avoiding being thrown to the ground.

She was a good rider but she still

retained her imagination. She knew that a rider thrown from a terrified horse risked being hurt not only from the fall but from the crushing of panic-stricken hoofs. Fear shot through her veins.

Chief was a powerhouse of violence — energy burst from its channels and running amok — a juggernaut out of control. She had no way of fighting him. She dug her feet deep into the stirrups and buried her fingers in the long black mane, trying desperately to hang on. She did not know how long the terrible turbulence lasted. But gradually calmness returned, the world steadied itself, life started to go on. She released her hands from the mane. They were wet and trembling. In her fear she had pulled out great tufts which lay in a sticky mass across her palms. Her body jerked and twitched in agitation.

She realised with swift compassion what dreadful fear the horse must have suffered. She lowered her exhausted body onto his neck and caressed him with her hands and voice. Gradually she became aware of Brio and his rider standing in silent contemplation just ahead of her. Phillippe did not enquire about her condition. He said simply, 'Well done.'

She looked at his face. It held no readable expression. She knew she had been put to the test.

Yet as they walked back to the stables she was not able to decide whether her competence in coping with the crisis represented a pass or a failure in Phillippe's eyes.

# 5

'Darling!' Vinnie shrieked, her eyes widening in fascinated horror, 'he put you on Chief! That horse is a crazy adolescent with a 3-litre engine and no brakes. What on earth was he thinking of?'

'I don't know,' Janet said slowly.

They were sharing tea together in the cottage before Janet's hour of teaching at 4 p.m. Vinnie had been shopping in preparation for her marriage. Parcels spilling over with clothes and shoes lay all over the room. She had brought scones and cakes from a local bakery and heaped them unceremoniously on a paper bag on the table. 'Eat, my sweet!' she commanded. 'I know you'll be positively ravenous and I wouldn't want you to fade away now you've come along to brighten my life with your adventures.'

They munched together, curled up on the sofa.

'So where did you go?' Vinnie asked, pulling a pair of ridiculously frilled french knickers from a bag and eyeing them critically.

'Oh — across the fields. We went to look at an old house — Greenfern Hall.'

Vinnie suspended her attack on the food and lingerie and stared at Janet.

'My God!' she exclaimed, 'that's a positive deathtrap for horses, full of bats, spooks and goodness knows what. Even the best horse would get scared crazy there!'

'Yes' — Janet agreed, 'I know.'

She told Vinnie the whole story. Vinnie was appalled.

'Oh — Phillippe! He's a naughty boy,' she said. 'I must speak to him.'

'No!' Janet said in alarm.

'The Baron — darling — would have the proverbial pink fit if he knew.'

'Yes. Please don't say anything,

Vinnie. I'm too new to have my boat rocked.'

Vinnie laughed. 'All right, sweetie pie. Now just look at all my purchases. All guaranteed to drive Peter J. S. positively berserk at the post-nuptials!' Janet noted that Vinnie's nightdresses and négligées cost as much as the whole of her mother's pre-wedding buys put together. Vinnie was just that sort of girl. Wherever she went she would get all the lollipops and no one would object.

Vinnie lay back on the sofa, licking buttery fingers.

'I went for a hack, too, today,' she said, 'on good old Yorkshire Pud. He's a darling. Phillippe's entering him for the Prix Musicale at Aachen next year.'

'I'm impressed,' Janet said. 'Do you ride all the top-class horses?' she added curiously.

'Oh, gracious no, darling. Just the understudies. Brio's the star. No one gets to ride him but Phillippe. I just have a sit on the also-rans now and again.'

Janet wondered about Vinnie's riding skill. She made it sound the most natural thing in the world to take out a top-class dressage horse for exercise. Janet would have given her eye teeth for a ride on one — and she was a reasonably accomplished horsewoman.

'Vinnie,' she asked, 'is Phillippe a relation of yours?'

'Not really, pet.' Vinnie considered her with languidly amused eyes. 'Do you want the family tree?'

'Well — yes,' Janet admitted.

'Here goes then. My grandfather and the Baron were great friends. They were both Austrian and came to settle in England and married delicious English roses. Their offspring in turn married and still remained friendly, so that the four grandchildren feel a bit like cousins.'

'Four grandchildren?' Janet asked.

'Goodness, darling, you are curious. I positively die with tedium listening to other people talk about their families. Yes, Phillippe has a sister — Jeanne.'

'Jeanne Géraudin — the famous grand prix rider.'

'That's right, sweetie.'

'But she's French!'

'Yes — so is Phillippe — half-French. Their mother Stephanie was French and never came to live in England. She was widowed in the war. Phillippe came to live with the Baron a few years after she remarried.'

'Oh,' said Janet, trying to take everything in.

'The dear old boy — he's had his trials. A widower at forty — only son killed in the war and a daughter who lives thousands of miles from him — no wonder he takes refuge in food!' She picked up a rum truffle and attacked it like a dainty squirrel. 'Can't say I blame him — after all, what is there in life apart from the stomach?' She rolled her eyes wickedly, indicating that there was an awful lot more!

'You're going to be late, sweet

hard-working girl,' Vinnie said, eyeing the clock and snuggling deep into the sofa.

Janet flew out of her chair, crammed on her hard hat, picked up her riding whip and tried hard to look professional.

'Don't worry, angel — it will only be some jolly fat-bottomed little girls, wide-eyed about ponies because they haven't got round to thinking about the male gender on two legs.'

Janet laughed, but later was thoughtful as she walked to the stable block to meet her pupils. Had Phillippe deliberately set out to test her courage and stamina? Surely he would not have planned to place her in a dangerous situation. She could have been injured — put out of riding action for weeks. She rejected the idea as preposterous but she could not push away a feeling of uncertainty that was almost thrilling in its gnawing intensity.

Vinnie was wrong about jolly little

girls. Two solemn-eyed boys stood waiting for her in the stable yard — obviously miserable with apprehension.

A small dark-eyed woman stood with them.

'Miss Holt,' she said in a brisk, friendly manner as Janet approached. 'I'm Alexa Firth and these are my sons, Graham and Stuart.'

The boys offered their hands gravely to Janet, staring at her with undisguised trepidation.

'They had a couple of lessons last year but it was rather a disaster,' Mrs Firth told Janet quietly. 'The young woman who taught them was over-optimistic about what they could do. Stuart had quite a bad fall.'

'Don't worry, I'll take things gently,' Janet said reassuringly. 'We'll soon build up their confidence.'

Alexa Firth smiled. She had beautiful soft brown eyes. They looked vaguely familiar.

'Good!' she said. 'The Baron told me

he had just the person to bring them on!'

A warm glow of pleasure settled over Janet as she took the children into the teaching arena. She told them about the ponies and how they liked to be talked to and fondled, how to tighten up the girth under the ponies' bellies, how to run the stirrups down and adjust them. By the time the boys were mounted up, their fear had been displaced by interest and curiosity.

She gave them a gentle lesson, aiming to give them the idea that they were in charge of the ponies rather than the other way round. She could tell they were relaxed and enjoying themselves. She was already planning how to develop their skills in the weeks ahead.

Alexa Firth sat in the spectators' gallery and smiled approvingly. At the end of the lesson when the boys had gone to untack the ponies she told Janet how relieved she was that the lesson had gone well.

'I did not want them to come again,'

she said. 'My brother booked the lessons as a birthday present for them. He felt sure they'd love it once they got going. And I think he was right.' She smiled warmly and patted Janet's hand. 'Actually he'll be bringing them sometimes, as I shan't always be able to manage it; in fact I was expecting him today — he must have got held up.' She looked down the lane as though she might conjure up the man in question. As if in response to her words a big saloon car rolled gently up the lane, seemingly devouring all the bumps.

A tall, broad-shouldered figure stepped out and walked up to them. He kissed Alexa's cheek lightly. His gaze travelled to Janet, and he grinned, brown eyes sparkling with amusement.

'Hullo, Janet!' he said in his mock grave manner, tilting his head slightly as she had seen him do before. She was a little taken aback.

'Hullo — Mr er — ' she was unsure how to address him.

'Max,' he said firmly. 'How are you?'

Unlike many people he waited for an answer to his question.

She was surprised not to feel embarrassed, recollecting the events of the previous night. Instead she found herself sharing his amusement. They both gave a little snort of laughter.

'I'm much better than I was, thank you,' she told him. 'The man with internal hammers has gone elsewhere,' she said, tapping her forehead, 'and my stomach has decided to go into the digestion business again.'

She was usually diffident about trying out a joke. She need not have worried, Max's face showed a perfect under-standing of her lightness of tone.

'You two seem to know each other,' Alexa said drily.

'We have met,' Max said, his face still alive with amusement. 'Yesterday, at a birthday party where the champagne was flowing rather freely!'

'Ah,' Alexa said, pulling a wry face, 'say no more.'

'Incidentally,' she told Janet, 'Max is

my brother — the kind uncle who's providing riding lessons.'

Janet realised now why Alexa's brown eyes had seemed familiar. Max must be a lovely uncle, she judged, thinking of his kind glance, the security of his large hands, the gentle humour in his expression.

He drew a brown bag with 'Thornlea Restaurant' written on it in gold letters from his pocket. 'For you,' he said to Janet. 'What you missed last night.'

The bag was full of the dainty brown almond biscuits she had been so disappointed not to eat. She was immensely touched. 'Amaretti!' she exclaimed. 'Oh, that's very kind!'

As she looked up at him she became aware of Phillippe's lithe figure crossing the stable yard. A thrill of piercing sensation rocketed through her body. She could hardly stop herself running to him, throwing her arms around him, telling him he was the most beautiful, desirable man she'd ever seen. He would tell her that the morning's hack had all been a terrible mistake, that he had only put her up on Chief to prove how skilled she was, how she could control this horse who only had to twitch his massive shoulders to unseat less experienced riders.

She pulled herself out of her mental cruising with a jerk. Max Thornton's brown eyes were looking at her enquiringly. He had followed the line of her gaze. She wondered if he guessed anything of her thoughts.

'See you next week,' was his parting shot. 'Keep off the champagne for a day or two!'

Alone again her elation subsided. The day's work was finished. An ache of homesickness pulled at her. She stood for a moment taking in the stillness of a summer evening, appreciating the expanse of bluey-green sky, fringed with coral-tipped white ruffles. In the fields the sheep lay tranquil and untroubled, gazing into space. In the air was a tangle of scents — drying hay, faint traces of animal excrement, creosote from a newly erected fence, and the warm smell of horses' bodies and hair.

She wandered down to the lower stable yard where all the top dressage horses were kept. She patted their necks and talked to them softly. Last of all was Brio. He moved away from her in agitation, his eyes full of alarm. She persuaded him to put his head down towards her. He flinched when she patted his neck, so she fondled his ears a little instead. Success! He rubbed against her for more, pushing the soft furry outer ear against her jacket. He started to push and nuzzle at her hip bone, push, push — more and more insistent.

'What are you doing, Brio?' she whispered. She glanced down. The brown bag with the gold writing hung out of her pocket. Brio was showing some anxiety to examine the contents. She took a biscuit out. He sniffed, he flapped his bewhiskered lips, he took and munched and wanted more.

What was it the Baron had said — if

only he knew how to give Brio pleasure; well, she might be able to tell him something in the morning! What a discovery!

She walked back to the cottage. The black Porsche came growling down the lane; Phillippe looked all set for an elegant evening out. He gave a brief wave, barely glancing in her direction. It cut her so that tears almost sprang to her eyes and a heaviness came into her legs.

'Cheer up,' Vinnie said when she saw her, 'you're just totally clapped out — nothing more than dying from exhaustion.' She made Janet lie in a bath of Dior scented oil and scurried about putting her purchases into drawers.

'Heavens!' she said, 'no point saving this lot up for the nuptials; might as well wear them now and get a fresh lot later!'

★ ★ ★

As the cool wet summer brightened into early autumn the Yorkshire hills surrounding the stables took on a warm, serene air.

Janet got into the habit of riding out early before breakfast either on the aptly named September Morning or on Little Nell for whom she had a great affection. The mare was quiet, yet responsive; she seemed to sense her rider's moods and was equally happy galloping with abandon over the stubble fields or trotting sedately down the stony bridle ways.

Janet loved these early September mornings when a glow, white and luminous, showed behind a thick veil of dripping mist. She admired the glittering gems of moisture on the bronzing leaves, the glazed and shimmering cobwebs stretched over gateposts and branches. The country air had a gentleness and purity about it, which could never be found in a city. Sometimes she loved it so fiercely she wanted to reach out and embrace it.

Her life had changed so much in those few weeks she found it hard to remember the girl who had set out from home with some new-found independence and a good deal of trepidation. Not only had she improved her riding technique, she had also experienced the loneliness of being separated from her family and the exquisite pain and excitement of being intensely and hopelessly in love.

For Phillippe had proved to be tantalisingly elusive. On occasions he gave her his brilliant smile and she basked in its warmth as though under a Mediterranean sun. He was an interested and sympathetic teacher and spent time in helping her over problems she encountered in her riding. He would discuss points of technique with her, looking deeply into her face as though she really meant something to him. Yet at other times he was aloof and casual — almost rejecting. She puzzled over this and eventually reached the conclusion that his coolness was somehow linked with his grandfather's presence, for it never occurred on the days when the Baron was not involved with her riding instruction.

But she was not quite sure how to interpret this observation. Did Phillippe resent his grandfather's eccentric approach to equitation, did he feel that his position as the main instructor was threatened? Or was there something else? Certainly the Baron appeared very pleased with her progress and he seemed positively fond of her. He gloated over his discovery of Brio's predilection for dainty almond biscuits and treated it as a little secret between them.

And Brio was coming on nicely. Phillippe worked with him regularly. Sometimes if Janet was about he would invite her to watch him and offer her criticism. She cherished these times for besides giving her the privilege of seeing a top-class horse and rider working together she sensed an intimacy between them. It was as though through asking for her criticisms that he was prepared to reveal his vulnerabilities to her. She felt this must be special as he normally presented himself as such a strong figure.

When Phillippe was relaxed, his horse went beautifully for him. Brio's movements were as fluid as waves sucking at the sand. His eyes lost their troubled agitation and softened into an alert expectancy as though he could hardly wait to respond to every fresh command. But occasionally the horse was ill at ease, ragged and jumbled up like an untidy-looking sky during changeable weather. It was on those days that Phillippe was tense, coiled up like a spring.

She wished Phillippe would give her the chance to find out more about him as a person. She felt that she never got anywhere near him. When he was in a dark mood he seemed enclosed, walled up inside his own feelings. But when he was cheerful and full of charming animation she got no closer. He simply radiated life and enthusiasm and refused to be drawn into any discussions that were not light in tone, matching his mood.

When she pursued her own lines of conversation and questioning he always pushed her deftly back to straighter and narrower paths, far away from the winding little lanes that led to personal thoughts and feelings.

'Do you have any hobbies, Phillippe?' she asked him one day as they walked together to the teaching arena.

He frowned. 'No,' he said, 'this horse business takes up all one's time, doesn't it?'

'Well, perhaps not all,' she said.

'You don't get far if you're not a hundred per cent involved,' he said curtly. 'It's all hard slog — even if you get nowhere!' he finished bitterly.

It was strange — she sometimes felt that he found no real joy in riding. He certainly underestimated his skills. For even though he was not a winner in top-class international competitions he had been placed second and third in lesser events and was generally recognised as a promising rider.

Vinnie was uncharacteristically reticent when Janet tried to quiz her about Phillippe.

'He's a gorgeous, handsome, spoiled darling,' she said. 'Don't touch him with a barge pole, pet. He's certainly one who might rock your boat!'

At other times Vinnie displayed a certain exasperation at Janet's continued admiration of a man who showed no signs of returning her interest.

'Look, sweetheart,' she said one evening, pouring a glass of wine for Janet when she came in from a gruelling day, 'he's only human for goodness sake. If you want him to take notice, stand up and be noticed.'

'What do you mean, Vinnie?'

'Well, why wait here until he snaps his fingers? We're in the 1980s, darling. Equality for all. Personally, I'm quite willing to recognise men as my equals, as some famous lady once said. The point is, why should you sit here like a flower on the wallpaper? Invite him for drinks, take him out to lunch. *Do* something!'

'Oh, Vinnie, I couldn't!??

'Why?'

'Well . . . '

'Well, what?' Vinnie looked at her with amusement from under her long black lashes.

'Well — I haven't the nerve to ask him here and I can't afford to take him out to lunch to the sort of place he'd appreciate. I just couldn't ask, I'm too shy — I'm not like you!'

It was quite true — Vinnie could get away with anything. No one ever put her down, she was never confused or crestfallen.

Vinnie ignored her observation. 'Go to the Thornlea,' she said, gesturing dramatically. 'Max'll give you lunch on the house.'

'Oh, Vinnie!'

Vinnie glanced wickedly at her friend. 'I bet he would. I've watched him talking to you after those super snappy lessons you give those spaniel-eyed little boys. He never takes his eyes off you.'

'Vinnie!' Janet said warningly.

'It's true,' Vinnie said dreamily, 'and he's such a beautiful man. That powerful body; he must be magnificent stripped — like a 17-hand hunter — all glossy rippling muscles.'

'You've had too much wine!' Janet said, laughing. But Vinnie was quite right about Max Thornton's eyes. He had the steadiest gaze of anyone she had ever met — sometimes it was almost disconcerting. She realised that it was a rare characteristic — to look at another person as though they had real importance. Other people spent a good deal of time talking to knives and forks and walls.

He often brought his nephews for their lesson and always thanked Janet courteously for her efforts with them.

He was unfailingly calm and pleasant, always interested to hear how she was progressing in her own riding skill.

He showed interest in other aspects of her life as well. 'Do you manage to see your family often?' he asked one day.

She explained that the weekends were busy so that it was difficult to get away.

'My mother visited me last week with her new husband,' she told him, laughing. 'I think she's very happy — not missing me much at all.'

A pang tugged at her heart as she spoke. She had not previously openly admitted this to herself, let alone to anyone else. Max Thornton was so easy to talk to, so gravely perceptive, that he seemed to draw out confidences before one had even begun to consider whether it was wise to confide or not.

He gazed into her face.

'Do you feel lonely ever?' he said.

She smiled with a faintly artificial sparkle. 'Oh no!' she protested, hearing her voice sound unnaturally brittle.

'I see,' he said. He looked faintly disappointed. She thought he must have seen through her pretence. No one else had considered her possible loneliness, and Max's voicing of it caught her unawares. She felt sorry that she had glossed things over.

Vinnie's continued gurglings of admiration for Max amused Janet. She could not help, however, thinking it strange that a girl about to be married should take such an interest in another man.

'After all, Vinnie,' she said, 'surely you're supposed to have eyes only for the groom-to-be.'

'Darling!' Vinnie shrieked, 'how boring life would be if one could only look in one direction. I've never been handicapped by tunnel vision and I don't intend to start now!'

Janet felt her face assuming a pinched and shocked expression — she tried hard to conceal it, but failed.

'You needn't look so disapproving,' Vinnie said archly, 'I just look — I don't touch — and it makes life a whole lot more fun.'

And Vinnie certainly had lots of fun. She was always being invited to join parties of laughing, prosperous-looking young people. She went out to restaurants, to the theatre, to lunches and dinners. She was everyone's favourite. Janet was invited along sometimes and very occasionally she agreed to join a party. But her days were tiring and often she simply preferred to rest at the cottage.

On one such evening in late September she had just settled down with a book when there was a sharp tap on the door.

She was surprised to see Phillippe's lean figure framed in the doorway. Her heart began to thunder in her chest and blood rushed to her cheeks.

'Would you like to come in?' she asked politely.

He hesitated. 'Well,' he said, 'just for a moment. I mustn't stay long.'

'I was having a quiet evening

reading,' she said, a little lost for words at meeting him alone in such a different setting from the business-like atmosphere of the teaching arena. He seemed unlike his usual, assured self — as though he had had a surprise — a shock even.

He stared around, his eyes travelling curiously over the furniture as though searching for something.

'Would you like a drink?' she asked, wondering what there was in the cupboard besides sherry.

He frowned a little, then smiled. 'Yes, please.'

'Sherry?' she enquired hopefully.

'Fine.'

He seemed disinclined to help the conversation along. She could feel him staring at her as she got the glasses out. They tinkled together as her hands shook with emotion. She was sorry she had her old jeans on and a couple of sweaters to keep out the chill. She felt lumpy, unattractive and insignificant.

He, on the other hand, looked, as Vinnie would say, positively edible. He had not yet lost his tan, which looked even more exotic than before in the context of a damp autumn evening. He reminded Janet of beautiful paintings or sculptures in exclusive shops — utterly perfect, perfectly simple and simply out of her reach. She felt that these moments whilst he was sitting there on her sofa drinking Vinnie's golden oloroso were the most precious she had ever experienced. It was as if the rest of the world were far away and just she and Phillippe were together surrounded by a warm circle of golden light as dusk grew outside and the colour drained from the sky.

'The Baron has been disagreeing with me about the horses I've been putting you on,' he said suddenly.

'Oh,' she said with interest.

'I think he feels you're not getting a fair crack of the whip,' he said with a smile. His composure was returning gradually. He paused and tapped his glass with one of his slender fingers. A vein twitched in the back of his hand and a shaft of longing twitched in Janet's throat.

'And what do you think, Phillippe?' she said softly, lingering over his name as though savouring a rare brandy.

'I think he might be right,' he said, turning his glass and examining the glimmers of light hovering in the golden liquid.

'Oh,' she said again uselessly, cursing herself for her lack of conversational sparkle.

'Yes,' he said thoughtfully. 'He might just be right.'

He sipped his sherry. Janet sipped hers.

A silence grew between them. Janet could think of nothing to say, nothing to ask him, nothing to make him stay. Her cheeks burned and the blood roared in her ears. Her palms were clammy with humiliation.

He seemed unperturbed. 'We'll sort something out tomorrow,' he said, draining his glass and standing up purposefully.

Janet watched helplessly as he got out his car keys and prepared to leave.

'Are you going out?' she asked in a deliberately casual way.

'Yes,' he said, as he walked towards the door, 'want to come?' His tone bettered hers for casualness.

She could not have been more surprised if he had thrown himself at her feet and asked her to marry him. He could not mean it. She was too dull for him, she had no means of amusing him.

'Oh — I'm not dressed for going out,' she said, as though that mattered!

'Oh, well!' he shrugged, 'another time perhaps. See you in the morning! Thanks for the sherry.'

She watched the tail lights of the car bobbing over the cobbles and listened, straining her ears until the last note of the engine had died away into the dripping air.

She walked around the room with

every nerve in her body raw and aching. Her heart felt sodden with grief. Why on earth didn't I say yes. How could I have been so stupid. How could I have complained about not being dressed properly, like some vain girl who's only bothered about how she looks. The questions tumbled round and round in her head until it throbbed. She had rejected him — the one man in the world she most wanted to be with. He had asked for her company and she had refused it.

She could hardly bear to be alone with her own stupidity. She telephoned home but there was no reply.

Vinnie's right, she thought. I'm just a useless, wilting wallflower as far as men are concerned. He won't ask again and I don't deserve him anyway.

# 6

In the morning she had to wear grey eye-shadow to conceal her pink-rimmed eyes. 'Ugh!' she said in disgust, eyeing her reflection in the bathroom mirror.

Her spirits were low as she took Little Nell up to the teaching arena. The day was as dark as granite and a bitter chill hung in the air.

She was startled to see the Baron stalking round the arena in a thoughtful, distracted kind of way. He rarely came to the early part of her lessons, usually dropping in part way through, interrupting the flow of Phillippe's instructions and generating an atmosphere of suppressed irritation. Phillippe, however, was nowhere in sight.

She was fond of the Baron. His deep, genuine kindness inspired confidence.

So she was pleased to find him waiting for her.

'My dear!' he greeted her. 'A very unpleasant morning. We must do something very, very nice to cheer it up.' He fondled the mare and gave her a mint-flavoured chocolate crisp which he scraped out in little bits from his jacket pocket.

'Up you get,' he commanded, 'and put her through a few simple exercises whilst I decide which of my prize horses we're going to try you on.'

She obeyed instantly, swinging Nell away to the edges of the arena and walking her around gently. She recalled all the Baron's advice — remember that the walk is the most suitable gait for creating a peaceful and receptive mood in the horse. Let the horse find her balance and then give her as much freedom as possible. The rider must keep the seat supple, make sure the head, shoulders, hips and heels are all vertically aligned; then relax — enjoy the precious, secret communication between horse and rider.

She smiled at that last maxim. It did not matter that the Baron had his hawk-like eye on her, that Phillippe had joined him and was watching with sharp appraisal. She could not help enjoying herself, feeling the horse's quarters move underneath her, seeing the glossy neck ripple with movement and knowing that she was in full control.

'At last,' the Baron said when the exercises were completed, 'you are learning not to fight against pleasure. Now,' he said with purpose to Phillippe, 'shall we try her on Baba . . . or should we see what she can do on Princess?'

Janet was thunderstruck. Baba was a superb horse — but Princess! She was second only to Brio. She had only ever seen Phillippe ride her. She turned her eyes anxiously towards him, a little afraid of his reaction. But no flicker of displeasure showed in his face.

'Why not?' he said evenly. 'I'll go and fetch her.'

The grey mare, standing proudly in the arena before Janet mounted, was more than worthy of her name. There was a dignity about her, a majestic composure that was almost daunting.

'Do not be afraid of her,' the Baron said gently. 'She is indeed a princess — but you, my dear, can be a queen when you are riding her if you treat her properly.'

Once Janet had the horse working obediently she realised why it is said that every rider needs a top-class horse to complete his or her education. On Princess she felt that all she had ever learned about riding fused into a unity of perfection. She felt that they could not go wrong, they were triumphant and invincible. She did not want to stop — wanted to go on and on, married to the movements of this superb creature who seemed to respond to the merest trembling thought of a command.

At the end of the session the Baron's eyes looked a little cloudy.

'I remember,' he said softly, 'that joy

I saw in your face. That's all behind me now, I'm afraid. Sad to grow old,' he murmured, 'so sad.'

He turned and walked away into the grey morning.

'Coffee time!' Phillippe said, matter of factly, breaking the mood. Then . . . 'That was good. There are a few points I want to discuss, but basically it was good.'

Janet glowed. Warmth spread through her body. The morning was magic. Life was wonderful.

Phillippe patted the grey mare. 'She's not so bad, this one,' he said. He looked at Janet, his eyes alight with amusement. 'Rather like getting out of a Vauxhall Chevette into an XJS automatic?' he suggested with unusual playfulness, tugging at the horse's ears.

'Or a Porsche?' she ventured gaily.

He declined to comment. His features rearranged themselves into a stern set.

She sighed. She seemed to have a knack of saying the wrong thing to him.

She must learn to be more sensitive, not to assume a familiarity which existed only in her dreams.

Vinnie shared generously in Janet's pleasure.

'Super, darling,' she said. 'Recognition at last. About time someone other than Phillippe got a share of the goodies,' she added with her sly chuckle. 'It'll get him off his comfortable perch on the laurels.'

'Oh dear!' Janet said, seeing new worries looming ahead.

'Haven't you invited him out yet?' Vinnie asked, rolling her eyes. 'That should take his mind off horses!'

'Oh, Vinnie,' Janet sighed. 'I seem to do everything wrong when he's around. Sometimes I feel as if I'm talking to him from a box at the bottom of the sea for all the contact I'm making!'

Vinnie screeched with delight — 'Oh, super imagery, darling.'

'No,' Janet said dismissively, 'I read it in a book. It's not original.'

'You're far too modest,' Vinnie said. 'I

can't even remember a good line from a book, let alone quote it.'

'No, you just think up a few of your own to compensate,' Janet said gloomily.

'Look!' Vinnie said, staring at Janet with ferocious exasperation, 'it's about time you did some stocktaking of your assets. You're a very talented, attractive person and I'm sick of hearing you running yourself down. In fact if you don't stop I shall pack up and leave!' She halted abruptly and they grinned at each other.

'That reminds me,' she said, 'I'm going away at the weekend to the in-laws to be.'

She pulled a face. 'Could be grim, pet. Mother Villiers isn't my idea of an exciting companion. She'll be doing the Flag Day for Lifeboats, or whatever, wearing her tweed underwear and her moustache. Still, Pa's O.K. when he's had a few pre-dinner whiskies.' Vinnie looked as though she were trying to put a brave face on things.

'But what about Peter?' Janet asked.

'Oh, still in Europe.' Vinnie sounded vague.

'Don't you ever see him?' Janet was becoming quite curious.

'Lots of time for that, darling. Years and years when we're married.'

Vinnie disappeared to cram some of her beautiful clothes in a case.

Janet pondered. It was Friday. A whole weekend without Vinnie was not a happy prospect.

She telephoned her mother. It would be just possible to dash home and back on Sunday if she could persuade one of the young students to look after her horses. Suddenly it seemed important to go somewhere where she was known and valued and important.

Her mother sounded excited. 'Are you all right, dear? You haven't been injured at all, have you? How's that young man you told us about?'

Janet prepared to answer but there was no opportunity.

'Guess what? Harry's taking me away

this weekend to London. We're going to see a show and do all the museums. I'm so thrilled. He only told me at breakfast, gave me the theatre tickets with my morning cup of tea. Isn't it *romantic?*'

Janet waited for the flood of words to abate.

'That's lovely,' she said, as warmly as she could manage. 'You must send me a postcard!'

So that was that!

Vinnie left at 5 o'clock and at 7 Janet was dining alone in the cottage on some left-over cheese flan and a pear. Loneliness settled around her like a cloak. She knew she should be sociable and go to the communal dining room where the students training to be riding instructors took their meals. But although they were only a year or two younger than she, the gap in outlook and interests seemed quite great. They made her feel rather old and out of place.

She sighed. The quietness of the

cottage deepened as the light faded outside.

The telephone seemed to tear the silence. Janet jerked so violently with surprise that her book fell to the floor. Her heart pounded. She began to hope that it was Phillippe. By the time she picked up the receiver she could not imagine how it could possibly be anyone else. Her disappointment on hearing Alexa Firth's voice was considerable but she managed to hide it.

Alexa, like her brother, was very polite. She asked a number of questions about Janet's health, riding progress and so on, whether she was tired or not. Janet answered mechanically. The letdown was so numbing that her voice felt heavy and laboured.

'I wonder if you would be free on Sunday,' Janet heard her say. 'John and I would be very pleased if you could come for a meal.'

Janet's spirits lifted instantly. It was so good to feel wanted!

'Oh, I'd like to very much!'

'Max is coming, too, it's his one night off,' Alexa laughed. 'He said he would call for you — about 7.30 — will that be all right?'

Of course it would be all right. When she put the phone down she found that the atmosphere of the evening had changed. The cottage seemed brighter, the silence less oppressive. She made some coffee and put the radio on.

By 10.30 she was tired but contented. She was soaking in a warm bath when the telephone rang again.

This time it was Phillippe. She couldn't believe it. Her heart leapt about violently like some crazy uncontrolled animal, dryness seized her throat. Pull yourself together, she told herself, you see him every day and your heart behaves fairly reasonably.

'Janet,' he said languidly, lingering slightly over her name so that her legs felt about to melt into ectoplasm. 'I was wondering if you could join me on Sunday. I'm meeting some friends for a drink. Nothing special, just a get-together at the local pub . . . '

Disaster! Catastrophe! In Janet's mind the dimensions of her ill luck surpassed those of anything she had come across in Shakespearian tragedy. Whoever was guarding her destiny was not showing great care about the finer details.

'Are you still there?' his voice said in lazy amusement. 'Is the suggestion so horrific you can't even consider it?'

She took a hold of her wayward emotions.

'Oh, Phillippe,' she said correctly, 'I'm afraid I've already accepted an invitation for Sunday.' She was horrified to hear herself sounding so prim, not how she meant to sound at all.

'That's O.K.,' he said cheerfully. 'No problem. Another time, perhaps.'

'Yes,' she said faintly. Surely he would never, never ask again. Who would — having been refused twice?

She was shivering violently as she replaced the receiver on its cradle. The coldness from the room crept through her skin to merge with the coldness inside her.

She went to bed. She turned first on one side, then the other. She got up at 2 a.m. and made some hot chocolate. It was 4 a.m. before she slept. At 6.30 it was time to get up and look after her horses.

# 7

When Max came to collect Janet he found her looking pale and fragile, with scoops of dark skin under her eyes.

He settled her into the velvety passenger seat of his new blue Rover with care. She smiled gently at him. The fire and spirit he had seen in her eyes previously seemed to have dimmed. Her body was drained and limp.

She had spent the last two days sparring with her conscience. A number of possibilities had travelled through her mind. She could invent an illness and decline the invitation. Alternatively she could be very direct and tell Alexa of the situation. The ideas were preposterous, of course, instantly rejected.

What would Vinnie have done she wondered. It was not hard to guess. She would simply have telephoned Phillippe to say, 'Darling, I was absolutely desolated to have turned you down again. Whenever are we going to get together to put things right? I'm free Tuesday and Wednesday and for ever — just name a day . . . '

Janet would not do it. She had picked up the phone on several occasions. Her hands had turned to slime, her courage had deserted her.

Phillippe had been coolly affable when he saw her the next morning. He made no mention of the phone call. She had not felt able to refer to it either. Goodness knows what he would make of that! She felt herself to be inadequate, gauche and totally uninspiring.

Max made a few polite enquiries then sat quietly, apparently absorbed in his driving. He turned towards her suddenly and smiled. It was not a smile of dazzle and brilliance like Phillippe's but beautifully warm, gentle and full of kindness. There was also a shrewd perceptiveness etched in the fine tracing of the lines around his eyes.

'Cheer up!' he said.

She turned sharply and stared at him. 'Do I look miserable?' she asked.

'Yes,' he said, laughing, 'and now you look fierce.'

'Oh, heavens — I'm sorry — I didn't mean to look either.'

'It's all right — doesn't matter!'

'No — I really am sorry. I didn't mean to take out my bad mood on you!'

'I'm used to it. My customers do it all the time,' he grinned at her, 'but I make *them* pay for it.'

She laughed with him and stretched her legs out in front of her in a gesture which indicated an abandonment of gloom.

'That's better,' he said. 'More like the young woman I'm used to seeing working wonders with my two nephews.'

'Oh, Max!' she protested, 'you certainly know how to cheer a person up.'

'Good!' he said, 'but I meant it quite sincerely.' Then, 'Are you ambitious?' he asked her.

'In what way?'

'Oh, careers — developing your skills — yourself as a person, that sort of thing?'

'Well — I suppose so.'

'Only suppose?' he said with mild challenge.

'No one's ever asked me quite like that before — I had to think about it.'

'Is that so?' he commented drily. She was not sure how to continue.

'Tell me about your childhood,' he said without warning.

She was amazed. No one ever asked her things like that either.

But by the time they reached Alexa's house, Max knew quite a lot about Janet's childhood and Janet was beginning to feel that she would enjoy the evening after all.

Alexa greeted them warmly, surprising Janet with a little hug.

The two boys were craning over the

banisters to catch the visitors' eye.

'Uncle Max — come up and say good night to us,' Graham hissed — Alexa threw them a stern glance as Max bounded up the steps.

'Oh, he does ruin them,' she sighed happily. 'He'll be reading them a story and slipping them some money before he comes down.'

She took Janet into a large drawing room where traditional oak furniture and flower-sprigged upholstery created a comfortable rather than elegant atmosphere. A balding man sat at a desk in one corner.

'John!' Alexa said, as though calling him from a great distance, 'our guests have arrived. I'm sure they would like a drink,' she added pointedly. Her husband regarded his wife gravely, and shook hands solemnly with Janet.

'Totally immersed in his research,' Alexa said to his departing back. 'He's a pet really!'

Janet was given a glass of sherry. Alexa chatted to her for a few minutes and then went to the kitchen to check on the dinner.

Janet found she had soon used up the reliable, basic supplies in her conversational store cupboard — the weather, the pleasantness of the room, the health of the children. John listened politely but answered in phrases of no more than a few words. He seemed quite content to sit in silence, sipping his sherry.

After what seemed an age Max joined them. 'I'll have a whisky, John,' he said pleasantly to his brother-in-law, who showed no signs of offering anything unless reminded.

'Ah!' John said heavily, getting up and going out of the room. Janet gave an involuntary sigh of relief. Max said nothing. Suddenly he winked — an unbelievably wicked wink, making her laugh out loud. When John came back Max began to tell them things, amusing snippets he had just learned from the boys, stories about his more eccentric customers. 'Do you know?' he said, 'I have one couple who come regularly and go through the menu twice.'

'You mean finish one dinner and start again?' Janet asked incredulously.

'That's right.'

'Goodness — it must cost a fortune!' Janet burst out and then wondered if the remark was in what her mother would term bad taste.

Max seemed amused.

'Very good for business though,' he said, his eyes twinkling.

John said in his weighty way, 'Is business good then?'

Max stretched out his long legs and regarded his brother-in-law thoughtfully. He twirled his glass round slowly.

'Yes — I think one could safely say that business is good. It's an absorbing thing, isn't it, work? How's the book coming along, John?' Max asked with interest.

It was as though a light were switched on in John's brain. He came alive. He began to outline the problems of writing a book on the growth of parliamentary power in seventeenth-century Britain. He lasted through the melon and would have persisted to the end of the pork casserole had his wife not made a gentle intervention.

'Darling,' she said, 'can someone else have a turn?'

He sank into silence.

'I have to invite people to come and eat with me quite often,' Alexa said. 'I can't compete with the Tudors and Stuarts all by myself. Can we think of something else to talk about?'

'Alexa is intrigued by all the action at the riding centre,' Max told Janet. 'She's longing to know what goes on behind the scenes.'

'Besides a lot of hard grind,' Janet said, laughing — 'I'm not sure there's anything else to know.'

Max raised his eyebows — 'Ah,' he commented, 'do I detect exemplary loyalty and discretion?'

Janet was puzzled. What was he getting at?

'I suspect,' Max went on persistently,

'that it is Mr Géraudin's performance that most intrigues Alexa.'

'Oh,' said Janet, feeling warmth rise to her cheeks. 'Why?'

'He's so variable,' Alexa said. 'I've watched him schooling those wonderful horses. Sometimes he seems brilliant and at other times the horses don't do a thing for him. He can get very angry,' she noted, with slight disapproval.

'Oh, but he's a magnificent rider,' Janet said, aware that she was charging to Phillippe's defence with no attempt at subtlety. 'It's not always possible to get a good performance from a horse and it's especially hard for Phillippe as he has to work under his grandfather's direction, which means he is restricted in following through a certain method.' Her cheeks felt as though they were generating as much heat as the radiant bar of an electric fire and her heart was thundering again. She took a gulp of wine.

Alexa looked impressed. Even John glanced at her briefly.

But Max was gazing intently at her, a look of contemplative appraisal in his eyes.

'So,' he said quietly, 'you're telling us that it is the horses rather than Phillippe Géraudin who are erratic?'

For the first time Janet sensed a faint stirring of anger towards Max Thornton. Who was he to judge Phillippe? He knew nothing of riding, nothing of the difficulties of being the grandson of the Baron von Bleiken. The word erratic was unduly judgmental and condemnatory. It jarred on her nerves.

Before she had the opportunity to formulate any kind of denial Alexa began to clear away, clattering the cutlery so that words were not needed to fill any silences.

'Can I help?' Janet asked, half getting up.

'Certainly not,' Alexa said firmly. 'You're here for relaxation — and there are two perfectly able-bodied men available!' She swept out bearing the plates.

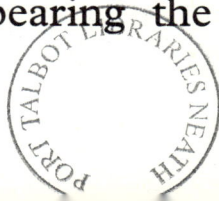

John sighed. 'Please sit down!' he said to Janet. 'My wife does not approve of women guests doing menial tasks.'

He gazed at the wine bottle and as though it were a novel idea, suddenly picked it up and refilled their glasses. 'Are you a feminist?' he asked Janet, 'keen on being called Ms and being independent and so on?'

Janet was relieved to be on safer ground again. She smiled. 'Well, I think I'm independent,' she said, 'but I don't know if I'm a feminist. I'm not worried about being called Ms anyway!'

'Good!' John said. 'We spend more time sorting out that wretched muz business at our department meetings than anything else. Damned waste of time — at least Alexa doesn't fuss about that. Can't think why she wants to go back to work now. We don't need the money and she's tied up enough with Open University studies.'

'She always was the able one in the family, John,' Max said. 'She hasn't tested herself out in the world since the boys were born. Perhaps it's time now.'

John said, 'Why should she need to test herself out in the world? She does a great job here.'

'Why write a book, John?' Max said evenly, 'when you do a great job as a professor at the university?'

Janet thought it was a neat point but John looked unconvinced as his wife dropped a raspberry pavlova in front of him and instructed him to share it out.

'I loathe cooking,' she said, 'especially when Max comes, he's such an expert.'

'But I never criticise!' he protested mildly.

'Do you cook at the restaurant?' Janet asked Max curiously.

'No — I just direct operations,' he said, grinning. 'But I cook for myself sometimes, for relaxation.'

'Heavens!' said Alexa. 'If you had to grind away every day feeding three ungrateful males, you wouldn't think it was relaxing!'

'No,' he agreed, 'I wouldn't.'

The evening passed quickly. Alexa

poured coffee and John brought out a bottle of malt whisky for them to sample.

At midnight Max announced his intention to leave. 'I'd better get Janet home before it gets really late,' he said, smiling kindly at her.

She sat beside him in the Rover, surprised at the contentment she felt. It had been a good evening after all.

'Not the easiest of men, my brother-in-law,' Max said. 'He's quite brilliant — very well known in his field. He's also enormously kind and about the most reliable person I've ever known.'

Janet felt the latter part of the description would have fitted the speaker quite adequately also.

'Is Alexa really unhappy just being at home?' she asked.

'Yes, I believe she is now. She's a fully qualified lawyer. She gave up a promising career to be a full-time mother.'

'I see,' Janet said. 'It's difficult, isn't it, for women?'

He turned slightly towards her. 'Yes,' he agreed, 'but life is difficult for everyone in some respect, don't you think? Perhaps even men!'

'You're making fun of me,' she chided.

'Not really. It's strange how things turned out. Alexa always wanted to be a lawyer but my parents tended to take a girl's ambitions less seriously. It was me they wanted to be the lawyer and I resisted like mad. I made sure not to do too well in any of my exams and left university with a very mediocre degree. My parents never really forgave me. They wanted a son who was a high-flying academic or professional. Being successful in business is second rate in their eyes.'

Janet was a little baffled. She could not imagine her own mother disapproving of Max in any way at all.

They sat in companionable silence as the car smoothly gobbled up the miles. The sky was thickly black and smooth as satin. A huge golden moon hung overhead and beyond it the darkness was pricked with trembling points of silver light.

Janet pressed her nose against the window as the car slowed down approaching a junction.

'Umm,' she said happily, 'it looks so beautiful out there I'd like to touch it.'

He pulled the car on to the grass verge bordering the narrow country road, leaving the engine running. Her window slipped down silently as he pressed a button on the control panel.

The night air was sweetened with the smell of damp grass and woodsmoke. She felt a surge of abandoned happiness, a sudden urge to jump out of the car and run along the verge in the moonlight. On every other occasion she would have dismissed the impulse. But tonight she felt strangely liberated.

She heard him laughing as she swung her legs out of the car. 'Just one minute,' she called. 'I'll come straight back!'

She slammed the door, then ran, jumped, skipped like an infant along the grass and inevitably stumbled over a resistant tuft and fell to her knees. She was still laughing as he came to her assistance.

'You crazy girl, what on earth are you doing?' he said, good-naturedly. Then as she limped on a slightly wrenched ankle, 'Are you all right?' he asked urgently.

'Yes — ' she said dismissively, 'I'm as tough as anything.'

He wedged her firmly under his arm. The contact with the solid warmth of his body was reassuring and unconflictingly pleasant. It seemed perfectly natural to relax and nestle against him without any sense of awkwardness.

'No harm done,' he said, having replaced her in the car and restarted the engine.

She felt disappointed that the evening had come to an end. She reflected on how much she had been amused and made to feel welcome — as though she really mattered.

She turned to Max and said contemplatively, 'You were drawing us out tonight, weren't you — John and me — making us talk about ourselves?'

'Well, it's one way of getting everyone to talk and keeping your secrets to yourself,' he said.

'Do you have secrets, Max?' she teased.

'Don't we all?' he replied gravely.

'Yes,' she said musingly — 'I suppose we do.' He was right, of course, no one knew of her intense longing for Phillippe — the sense of despair at her inability to move the relationship on to something more positive. She was on the point of confiding; of spilling the beans all over Max because she felt he could be trusted.

He interrupted her intentions.

'You were angry with me over dinner, weren't you?' he said.

She denied it, she did not feel now that it had been real anger.

'Yes,' he said firmly. 'I think I touched on a sensitive issue.'

'You're right,' she said sadly.

There was a silence.

'So,' he said softly, 'Phillippe's the one?'

'Yes.' She stopped uncertainly. 'Well, not really — I don't think he ever notices me.'

Max said nothing. She felt his understanding reaching out to her. A rush of warmth for him swept through her and she reached out and touched his arm. He smiled, his features pale and silvered in the moonlight. He made no further comment until they drew up outside the cottage.

Her mood of elation had vanished and she felt desperately tired. He knew she was alone and insisted on escorting her inside and ensuring that lights were switched on and no intruders lurking before he left.

She stood with him in the doorway, sorry that he was going.

'Well,' he said, 'I'll see you soon with

the boys, no doubt.'

'Yes,' she agreed. He stood pondering.

'You must come for a meal at the Thornlea again,' he said. 'You and Vinnie,' he added. 'I haven't shown you both the whole house yet.'

'Oh, Vinnie would love that!' she exclaimed.

'Would she?' he replied, staring at her.

'Yes!'

He seemed vaguely dissatisfied, still disinclined to leave.

'Well,' he said briskly, offering his hand, 'good night.'

It seemed too cold to part like that. She stood on her toes and put her hand up around his neck. He bent his head towards her and she kissed his cheek softly.

'Thank you,' she said — 'for everything.'

★　★　★

She waited until his car swung around the wall bounding the courtyard, then looked across to the stable block with an almost involuntary movement. In the offices overhead there was a light. She drew her breath in sharply — outlined against the window was Phillippe's lean figure, still and rigid. He raised his hand slowly to acknowledge her presence. The previous few minutes flashed through her brain. What would he make of that tender little scene?

Almost too tired to care, she locked the door and switched out the lights. A subdued but definite sound of human movement came from the bedroom at the head of the stairs. Momentarily fear jerked through her insides. A familiar auburn-haired figure threw open the door and stood dramatically at the top of the stairs.

'Late!' she drawled, wrapping a satin néglieée around her.

Janet collapsed against the wall which ran alongside the stairs.

'Oh, Vinnie, you scared me stiff. Whatever are you doing here now?'

'And whatever were you doing, sweet one, making love to the delectable Max on the doorstep at this time in the morning?'

'I was simply giving him a friendly goodnight kiss. There are occasions when men and women don't have sex on their minds.' Janet spoke rather irritably.

'Not many!' was Vinnie's comment. 'Where have you been, anyway?'

'I've been walking with him down lonely country lanes,' Janet said, her good humour returning.

'No! What happened?'

'I ricked my ankle!'

'Oh, darling — a walk in the moonlight with the scrumptious Max and all you can do is worry about your joints.' She paused. 'I suppose you'd already ravished him in the Rover, behind all that electrically operated tinted glass.'

'Sorry to disappoint you,' Janet said,

'but it was all just nice and friendly.'

'Ah,' Vinnie sighed, 'and I saw you married together in silent yearning — his hand caressing yours over the gear lever — only releasing it to change gear.'

'It's an automatic,' Janet said practically.

Vinnie gazed heavenward, 'Oh, the lost opportunities in life's rich pattern,' she mourned. 'You had it made, darling.'

'Vinnie,' Janet said sternly, 'I'm very tired and I want to go to bed and I want to know why you're not in Gloucestershire.'

Vinnie narrowed her eyes. 'Go straight to bed!' she commanded. 'Put on your woolly bedsocks and I'll bring you cocoa and tell all!'

However, there was not very much to tell, apart from the fact that Vinnie had been desperately bored with her future in-laws. Mrs Villiers had, as predicted, disappeared to sell flags on Saturday whilst her husband stalked around the garden tidying up stray leaves.

'He rushed out every time he saw one fall. I thought he might ring the parks department and instruct the gardeners to cancel all leave and come to the rescue. It would certainly have made a change if someone else had turned up.'

'Oh, poor Vinnie — I bet you were desolated without an audience.'

Vinnie slapped Janet's hand and the cocoa leapt in the cup and splashed on to the duvet cover. They both giggled.

'Nasty!' Vinnie said. 'There's no need for you to bite lumps out of my self-esteem, Ma Villiers already had a good go at that.'

'Shouldn't think she made any inroads,' Janet said.

'True, but she would keep raining on my parade when I tried a little wicked wit and there was no wine with the dinner!'

'Gosh,' Janet said, 'what deprivation.'

'Anyway it all got too much so I developed a sudden virus infection and left in a great show of sorrow.'

Janet regarded her, feeling a motherly expression settling on to her features.

'Oh dear!' she said, 'what about poor Peter?'

Vinnie pursed her lips — 'It'll be O.K.,' she said, 'it was hardly an international incident.'

Moonlight poured across Janet's bed as Vinnie switched off the light and prepared to go to her own room. 'By the way,' she said, 'I hear there are plans afoot for you to go to Holland at Christmas.'

Janet sat up. 'What?' she exclaimed.

'Oh gosh, have I put my dainty foot in it. Didn't you know?'

'Know what?' Janet said, in a frenzy of impatient curiosity.

'There's talk of you and Phillippe going to Holland for an international dressage competition.'

'But there isn't one at Christmas.'

'Yes there is, this year — it's a charity affair in aid of a worthy cause of some sort.'

Janet's head spun with the impact of the information.

'You mean I'm going to compete?' she said incredulously.

'That's the general idea, sweetie.'

'Oh God,' she exclaimed, sinking back on to the pillows.

A kaleidoscope of images revolved in her head. She saw Phillippe's brilliant, triumphant smile as he rode Brio. The Princess's rippling muscled neck rocking in front of her as the crowd applauded, rosettes pinned to her baggage on the way home, champagne corks popping. Then suddenly her thoughts shifted to another track, 'Vinnie, how did you know about it?' she asked.

'Oh' — Vinnie's voice came clear and unhesitant through the darkness, 'the Baron let it slip — he can't keep secrets, the darling.'

But you haven't seen the Baron since Friday, Janet thought. Why didn't you tell me then. The question continued to puzzle her as she lay waiting for warmth to reach through her limbs, and gradually it resolved itself into unconsciousness as she fell into a deep sleep.

In the morning Phillippe surprised her by requesting that she come up to his office before attending to the horses. He was very formally dressed as though about to go out to the theatre or a dinner party. There was an electric razor, its flex neatly wrapped around it, on his desk. It looked as though he must have spent the night in the office rather than returning to his house a mile away in the village. He gestured to her to sit down.

'Had a good evening?' he remarked, with a pleasant casualness that cut her like a razor.

'Yes, thank you,' she said meekly, as misery settled around her like a grey mist. She felt so different from the person she had been the previous evening. Then she had been confident, happy, witty even and a little reckless. Now she was dull, ineffectual and hopeless. And Phillippe, he looked so utterly desirable, so handsome and poised, she felt her heart would burst from wanting him. To be so near him and yet unable to reach out and feel the hardness of his finely tuned body was almost more than she could bear.

'There's a lot of work ahead of us,' he said briskly. 'I don't know if you've heard but there's to be a special dressage competition in Holland just before Christmas. It's going to be a spectacular affair at international level. Prizes donated by a German wine producer and all proceeds going to handicapped children — so you can imagine the interest and press coverage there'll be.'

'Yes,' she replied; it was hard to think of anything else.

'I'm going to take Brio — it will be good experience for him and I hope to get the Princess ready to compete as well.'

She waited expectantly for his announcement of her inclusion in the proceedings.

'That's where you come in,' he said. He gave her a cool look of appraisal, closely followed by one of his glittering smiles; she felt herself melting a little. 'I'll need all your help in getting her really stoked up to do her best.'

She glanced at him in dismay. Was he saying that her role was merely one of preparer and spectator rather than colleague and co-competitor as Vinnie had suggested.

'So, starting from today, I want you to school the Princess on your own. You're perfectly capable now. You don't need to be under my supervision all the time.'

'Do you mean you won't be giving me instruction any more?' she said, violent dismay clutching her stomach.

'Of course I don't mean that,' he said irritably. 'It's part of your contract anyway, apart from anything else.'

These were hardly words of comfort for Janet but she received them with commendable outward composure.

It was obvious that he considered the

conversation closed. She stared dumbly at him. Why couldn't she tell him what she had been rehearsing for the last couple of hours. Tell him how sorry she was that she had turned down his invitations, how she longed for another chance, how he was in her thoughts nearly all the time and how it had come about that she was kissing Max Thornton outside her front door at 1 o'clock earlier that morning. But it was all totally hopeless. She could no more express these thoughts to him than her mother could leave dust under the beds — it was simply unthinkable.

She went down to the stable yard — alone with her gloom. As she worked on Little Nell's glossy quarters with a dandy brush she heard the Porsche snarl its way down the lane and roar away into the distance. She leaned her head against Nell and sighed on to the velvety warmth of the horse's neck.

She worked four horses hard that morning, enjoying their differing rhythms and varying personalities. By lunchtime she was grimy and sweating; her hair sticking to her head underneath the constriction of the snugly fitting hard hat. Vinnie once suggested she should fit a steam valve to it, she generated so much heat!

She was walking Princess round the stable yard to cool her off before untacking her when she noticed a blue Rover coast up the lane and park by the fence. A flicker of anticipation that there would now be some relief of her despondency kindled inside her as she watched Max Thornton's long frame uncurl itself from the driver's seat. She raised her arm in a friendly wave as he came striding down the yard towards her.

'Hullo,' he said cheerfully, 'how's things?'

'Grim,' she said, pulling a wry face but at the same time thinking that perhaps things were not so bad after all. She looked at him and without warning felt a tremble of laughter working its way to her lips. He had been about to say something but he stopped and tilted his head in a familiar questioning gesture.

'If there's a joke can I join in?' he said with his usual good humour.

'Oh dear,' she said, the laughter escaping in spite of her efforts.

'What's so funny?' he said, grinning.

'You!' she said.

'Well, thanks!' he exclaimed.

'Oh, Max — I am sorry — it's just that you look so strange wearing that beautiful suit in the middle of our dirty yard.' Janet's sharp and observant eye had quickly taken in the soft sheen on the dark cloth, the exquisite cut of the jacket, the delicate fabric of the pale blue shirt and the very correct navy and blue striped tie. It struck her that he equalled Phillippe in terms of elegance, but his style was quieter and not so immediately striking. She looked down at herself, stained with sweat from the horse's flanks, her boots splashed with mud, her jacket flecked with horse hair. 'And here am I!' she exclaimed, still laughing, 'hot and scruffy, looking like . . . ' She ran her hand across her forehead, lost for words.

'Looking like you're getting a lot out of life rather than letting the world go by,' he commented.

'Oh — really?' she said, taken by surprise. She had almost expected an easy compliment, a cliché — you look charming or something of that sort.

'Yes!' he said firmly. 'Were you thinking of putting that horse somewhere?' he suggested, glancing at Princess who was standing quietly at Janet's side. 'I was hoping to have a word with you — that's if you can manage to look at me without collapsing with mirth?'

'I shall pull myself together,' she said. 'I don't usually carry on like this.'

'I'm sure you are a model of tact and politeness,' he said, adding pointedly — 'usually, that is.'

He waited until she put the horse in her box, then swung the discarded saddle and bridle over his arm despite her protests and carried them to the tack room — a cool dark room full of the smell of leather. They strolled out to the courtyard in front of the cottage.

'Will you come and have some lunch?' she asked. 'It's just a snack,' she said hastily, visualising assorted lumps of cheese sitting in the fridge.

He smiled and shook his head. 'No, I must get back to the restaurant, I've got the car loaded with supplies that are needed as soon as possible. I'm supposed to be working,' he said teasingly, 'hence the uniform!'

He paused and gazed at her, his brown eyes tawny and gold-flecked in the spear of white sunshine that had begun to pierce the clouds. She waited — puzzled but not at all disconcerted by his scrutiny. He reached into his pocket and brought out two tickets.

'A gift from a customer,' he said. 'Two seats for a recital at the cathedral next Sunday. The customer and his wife can't make it.'

'It should be very good,' he finished,

almost apologetically.

'Are you asking me to come with you, Max?' she said, sensing that for once he seemed to need help.

'Yes — I'd very much like you to. I did hesitate about asking — I don't want to make things difficult or queer the pitch so to speak. Just a friendly outing?' he looked at her quizzically.

She knew just what he was trying to tell her. 'There's no pitch to queer and I'd love to come,' she said warmly. And given a straight choice she would even prefer to go out with Max than with Phillippe. She would be able to relax; which was sometimes more agreeable than being at a fever pitch of excitement and uncertainty.

'Good!' he said. 'That's great! I'll pick you up at 7 p.m.' He got his car keys out. 'I must go,' he said urgently, 'there'll be a shortage of crisis proportions if I don't get all this stuff into the kitchen soon.'

'Go on then!' Janet said mischievously — 'I'm not stopping you.'

'Watch it!' he warned, aiming a playful punch at her nose. 'And consider warmth, not glamour, on Sunday,' he added, 'the cathedral's like a gigantic cold storage unit!'

She smiled, thinking that glamour was not in her repertoire anyway.

After lunch she decided to do some studying. She selected two hefty texts on academic equitation and laid them out on the pine desk in the sitting room. She made good progress and in an hour had covered four sides of foolscap paper with notes. She heard the gentle tap at the door with mild surprise — a greater surprise awaited her at the sight of the caller. It was the Baron, his kindly face smiling with his own curious blend of vagueness and shrewd assessment.

'My dear,' he said, 'will you invite me in? I shall not detain you long.'

She was a little troubled as though she had been summoned to the head teacher's office but she welcomed him with genuine pleasure even so.

He sat in the armchair nearest the fireplace — a bulky figure in his scratchy tweeds. His eyes examined the room, noting pictures, books and photographs. 'You have made a home here,' he said approvingly.

'My dear,' he went on, nodding his head rhythmically, 'I am a little concerned on your account.' He gazed steadily at a point just behind her head as though he were looking into the far distance.

'You have shown great promise as a rider — more even than I hoped for.'

She absorbed the news with happiness whilst he searched for his next words.

'But I worry for you,' he frowned. 'I want you to use this talent but I cannot quite see the right outlets for it.'

'I never expected more than I have learned or achieved here,' she said. 'I'm pretty realistic; I know I can't afford the sort of animal to take me into top-class competition work.'

'No,' he said. 'We talked of that, I

recall. But there are always sponsors. The dressage field may begin to attract interest, like show jumping and racing — who knows?'

She smiled wistfully. 'It's not on the cards now though, is it?' she asked.

He ruminated, his brow ridged with deep folds of thought — 'You need to become known,' he said, 'to bring your light from under the bushel.'

She laughed at his quaint turn of phrase. She began to have some idea of what was coming next.

'I want you to compete at the Christmas competition in Amsterdam,' he said flatly. He started to elaborate. '*I* want you to — but Phillippe is worried that you have too little experience to undertake such a challenge.'

'I see,' she said.

'How old are you, my dear — please remind me?'

'Twenty.'

'Yes,' he smiled, 'and he is twenty-six — a mere six years older.

'What difference does it make?' he

mused. He straightened his shoulders in a faint gesture of defiance. 'My dear — I have decided, in contrast with my usual principles to go against Phillippe's wishes and judgements on this occasion.'

'What do you mean?' she asked softly.

'I am simply going to overrule him. I make the final decisions still. You go to Holland and ride the Princess and Rum Baba. If I had my way — ' he continued, warming to his subject, 'you would . . . ' he stopped suddenly. 'No — I must not say any more . . . Please make sure you have an hour's schooling with each horse daily from now on and also take them out for quiet hacks in the lanes and fields. Let one of the best students ride Nell and the others. You must not tire yourself.'

It was hard to know how to reply to his words — behind which there was obviously so much feeling. She was very grateful to him, as one is to people who recognise and value those personal qualities one values in oneself.

'Thank you,' she said quite simply.

He got up stiffly. 'It will not be easy,' he said, 'any of it. I can see many difficulties.'

His words came back to her later when difficulties of a nature even he had not foreseen arose. He began to move towards the door.

'Will you stay and have tea?' she asked.

'Ah, how thoughtful! No, my dear. Tea is waiting at home. But I am afraid even my appetite is a little diminished at present.' He sighed and patted his stomach ruefully. 'It will pass,' he said. 'It will pass!'

Vinnie had no such reservations about food when she returned from a long hack on Rainbow. She had tied him up to a post in the village like something from a Western film and bought up what seemed to be a substantial proportion of the local baker's goods for tea.

'I've got two steaks for dinner as well

and a bottle of Beaujolais,' she said. 'We need it. Our lives have a sordid and tedious quality at the moment that no one should have to bear without some consolation.'

Janet did not disagree. She set about the food with vigour and whilst eating told Vinnie about her interview with Phillippe, about Max and finally about the Baron.

'Goodness — I only have to leave you a minute and your life is full of drama,' Vinnie said. 'I'm dying with envy.'

Janet smiled.

'How can you be so calm?' Vinnie shrieked.

'What do you expect me to do?'

'I can't think. But you shouldn't take an invite from Max so casually!'

'I'm not casual. He's just nice — a friend.'

'Oh Lord!' Vinnie groaned. 'He's the most fantastic man around for miles, he's absolutely loaded, supposedly as pure as the driven snow, wedded to the restaurant and totally dedicated to building up treasures here on earth. In short, to complete the biblical illusions, he's divine and all you can do is think he's a nice pal when he asks you out.'

Janet pursed her lips. 'Sorry,' she said.

'You're not still mooning over Phillippe?' She snapped a little and then stopped to check with Janet's expression. 'Yes, you are! You're crackers!'

'Well,' Janet said helplessly and quite irrelevantly, 'he isn't having an easy time at the moment, is he?'

'Rubbish,' Vinnie scoffed, 'he's about as psychologically sensitive as a jumbo jet, and it's time you stopped gawping at him as though he were the crown jewels — it doesn't do him any good. Cross him off the list, pet!'

'O.K.' Janet said, smiling. 'Look, Vinnie, what shall I wear on Sunday?'

'Ah, now that is a problem I like to solve,' Vinnie commented with relish. She snapped her fingers. 'I have it,' she said triumphantly. 'The black velvet skirt — glam and warm too — the plain silk shirt and a super Paisley shawl to drape around and snuggle into. Max will be able to get inside it too if things hot up!'

'Good!' said Janet — 'except I haven't got a velvet skirt or a Paisley shawl.'

'No problem, my sweet!' Vinnie dashed off, her long auburn curls swinging. The black skirt was flung ludicrously around her neck when she returned and the Paisley scarf knotted at her waist trailed dramatically on the floor.

'Vinnie — ' Janet said helplessly. 'It won't fit me. Your legs are about a foot longer than mine.'

'Quite — but the rest will do — we'll just chop off a lump at the bottom.'

Janet's sense of thrift suffered a terrible shock at these words.

'You can't!' she said in forbidding disbelief.

'I can and I will!' Vinnie said — and she did. Within minutes the skirt was shorn of several inches and Vinnie was pinning up what was left.

'You're mad!' Janet said. 'I never met anyone like you.'

'You couldn't have said a nicer thing, darling. I love to be called unique.'

Janet slipped on her cream silk shirt and arranged the shawl over her shoulders. It was in a soft yet heavyish material and settled around her as though it had been poured on.

'It's cashmere,' Vinnie said, tweaking at its fringed end, 'so don't do anything too sinful with it, I may want to wear it again.'

Janet looked disbelievingly in the mirror. Her skin looked creamy and glowing against the rich and varied textures of silk, velvet and cashmere. The colours in the shawl formed an autumn bouquet of russet and coral flowers which brought out an answering warmth in her cheeks, enlarged her eyes, emphasised the peachiness of her lips. For the first time she sensed what is like to feel truly desirable, that it would be a privilege to be touched, caressed, made love to. An involuntary smile curved on her lips.

'Sexy!' Vinnie commented flatly.

Janet raised her eyebrows and played things down a little.

'Not too glamorous?' she enquired archly.

'Not at all, darling. Understated elegance, as they say in the magazine. All you need are the mink-lined knickers to guarantee full warmth. Thermal underwear is absolutely out — the most dreadful turn-off for every-one.'

'I don't have either,' Janet laughed, 'so you needn't worry.'

As the week progressed she began to feel grateful that there was something to look forward to at the end of it, for the days became infused with an unresolved tension, an insistent disquiet.

The Baron retired to bed with an undiagnosed ailment. He refused to have the doctor and put himself on a diet of bread and milk. Vinnie said she could never remember his being ill before. It meant, of course, that Janet had to carry out his instructions in his absence, whilst Phillippe treated her with a polite disapproval that was infinitely more chilling than outright hostility. He went through the motions of giving her lessons as usual, but he ceased to instruct in any positive way; he merely watched with cool appraisal, occasionally offering a word of praise or indicating disapproval. It made no difference whether he applauded or rebuked, his tone was equally disinterested in either case. She became quite used to it. She felt she must have grown a thick emotional coat for she seemed to cope without undue distress. She sensed that the situation could not last, that there must be some resolution of the issue but whether it was to be pleasant or painful, she could not guess.

On Friday evening Vinnie invited three of the trainee instructor students to the cottage for drinks and supper. They arrived fresh-faced and jolly at eight o'clock and fell into easy horsey conversation with Vinnie, discussing the various mounts they had ridden that afternoon. They all hoped to qualify for instructor status within the coming months and then get permanent jobs as teachers in stables nearer their homes. One girl had two first-class jumping ponies of her own and hoped to mix competition work with freelance teaching.

Janet listened to their lively chatter with interest. She judged that she far excelled all three girls in riding skill, but wondered whether it would make any difference in the end.

'We really shouldn't talk horses all the time,' Vinnie exclaimed suddenly. 'Too dull!' Janet felt vaguely apprehensive as to what might be coming next. Vinnie had a demonic gleam in her eye.

'Janet's going to a wildly expensive charity concert at the cathedral on Sunday night,' she announced. There was a dramatic pause, and then punch-line, 'With Max Thornton!'

Janet winced with embarrassment. 'I'm sure they don't even know who you're talking about,' she said primly, feeling as though her voice was struggling through a mouthful of plums.

'Oh, I do!' one of the girls said. 'He owns that fabulous Thornlea restaurant. My parents took me there for a meal last time they came up.'

'He's super,' another added. 'Such sexy eyes — I bet he's fantastic in bed!'

'Must be worth a bomb!' They all seemed to want to join in.

Vinnie sat back smiling, looking as though she had laid a golden egg.

They all sighed in girlish ecstasy. Janet felt very annoyed. Their remarks in some way reduced Max to a trivial level, cheapened and coarsened the way she thought about him. She noticed the girls looking at her with a kind of awe as though she were something special. It really was too bad.

'Oh, come on, Janet, pet!' Vinnie crooned. 'I'm beginning to think you fancy him just like all the rest of us.'

Janet regarded her thoughtfully. 'No,' she said slowly, 'no, I don't.' And it was true, she truly did not fancy him in the casual way they were suggesting. A tenderness for him had grown in her heart which precluded such superficial emotions.

Vinnie said, 'Ah, he is indeed a perfect gentleman, not to be taken lightly, as Janet rightly suggests. There are too few of them about!' She winked a slow, outrageous wink at Janet, who stared fiercely back at her; daring her on no account to go further.

'Of course,' Vinnie said airily, 'one must consider what a true gentleman consists of. How should he be defined?'

Her audience looked a trifle non-plussed. It was obvious that she was going to answer the question herself.

'A gentleman,' Vinnie said, gurgling, 'is someone who says 'I do beg your pardon' as he tramples you underfoot on the promotion ladder.'

Janet could not avoid laughing.

'You read that in a magazine!' she said accusingly.

'No — I concocted it on my own and here's another. A gentleman is someone who sends his wife flowers three times a week when he's having an affair with another woman.'

There was some general merriment. They awaited Janet's comment. She was thinking that a gentleman was, in fact, someone gentle. Someone who protected you, but only when you needed it, liked you because you were a woman and respected you because you were a person. Someone who made you feel relaxed enough just to be yourself. She frowned a little; inside her the well of self-knowledge was stirring but it was still enclosed, so that she could not see into its dark waters.

'Janet,' Vinnie called, 'have you gone into a trance?'

'Oh,' she said, anxious to be rid of the interested eyes on her, 'I suppose someone who opens doors for you and that kind of thing.'

'Oh, my lord!' Vinnie said. 'All those labours to bring forth a flea!'

Janet escaped to make coffee. A vague disquiet shivered in the air around her. In her head, coloured fragments seemed to glide in a jumble of uncoordinated colour. A feeling of almost unbearable expectation was lodged in her stomach and limbs so that she could hardly face drinking the coffee she was making. She had a sense almost as strong as certainty that a storm was about to break over her head, but its nature continued to elude her, so that the clouds just built up with a grim and threatening force.

# 8

It was the next day when the storm broke — not from an unexpected source, but in a manner which left Janet weak with appalled amazement.

She had her lesson with Phillippe in the morning as usual, exercised and schooled the horses as instructed by the Baron and returned to the cottage around six o'clock, tired but satisfied. Vinnie had already gone out for the evening leaving a perfumed trail of garments scattered over the landing.

Janet telephoned home.

'Oh, love, it's so nice to hear your voice,' her mother said. 'When can you get home for the weekend? The house is all finished, we want to show you everything.'

Eventually they fixed on a date just before Christmas when Janet would be able to take a long weekend and the main part of the Christmas holidays. She chose the dates carefully, making sure they did not conflict with those of the dressage competition. She wanted to feel she was available should any opportunities arise for competing. But she made no mention of it to her mother.

'I'll have to be back on Boxing Day,' she explained. 'We take it in turns to have overall responsibility for the stables on Bank Holidays.'

'Oh, I see, dear,' Mrs Holt said doubtfully as though she thought it all a little unnecessary.

'How's that young man you told us about?' she went on carefully.

'Fine,' Janet said, with answering care.

'Have you been anywhere exciting, dear?' her mother asked tactfully without mentioning any names.

Janet told her about the visit to Alexa's. She did not mention Max, however, or the proposed visit to the concert the next day. It seemed to make her social life sound unduly complicated.

'Well,' her mother said with undisguised sympathy, 'I'm sure someone will turn up for you soon, dear!'

Janet felt annoyed that her mother put such stress on romantic involvements and appeared to play down her working achievements. She got out her notes on academic equitation and thumbed through them in a desultory fashion to ease her irritation. As she read, a thought suddenly struck her. She must try it out immediately. She threw on her quilted anorak and ran down to the stable yard. The students were busy feeding the horses.

'Jenny!' she called to one of the girls, 'has the Princess been fed yet?' The girl shook her head.

'Good,' said Janet. One couldn't ride a horse that had just been fed. 'I'm going to ride her for half an hour so I'll feed her when I've finished.' The girl looked at her curiously at first, then with relief that she was not going to delay her.

The Princess showed no surprise or resentment at being saddled up so late in the day. Janet led her up to the school and made her stand whilst she fumbled in the blackness for the levers to operate the floodlights.

She warmed her up with some sedate walking, talking gently to the mare's pricked ears as they relaxed together into rhythmical harmony. Then she slipped her into a simple sequence of dressage exercises, attending carefully to the movement of the horse's front legs and using only a very small area of the school in an attempt to achieve perfect control. She concentrated hard on the point the book had made about the use of a small space, wondering how long the Princess would tolerate restriction of movement in the quest for precision.

Without warning a drawling voice slid into the quietness of the arena. 'Working late?' it said. 'What dedication!'

Phillippe stood at the door, fit and supple-looking in a blond-coloured leather jacket. He walked towards her and came to stand at the horse's head.

'That was good!' he said softly. 'You really do have talent.'

She stared at him in fascination. She had never seen him quite like this before. His smile was as brilliant as a diamond, a muscle in his jaw plucked at the skin as though a bird's wing were fluttering there. He ran his hand under the horse's belly. 'She's very warm,' he said. 'Have you finished with her?'

'Yes, I suppose so,' she said faintly.

He held out a hand to steady her arm as she jumped to the ground and then pulled the Princess's reins over her head and told her to stand. There was a moment of stillness. Janet felt impelled to turn and look into his eyes. They were almost navy-blue under the fluorescent lights; they seemed to pierce her with their sharp fire.

'You're different from the others,' he said. 'Not just a little rich girl with the smell of horse up her nose.' He spoke with intensity, his voice low and caressing.

She trembled under his gaze, at the sound of emotion in his voice. And yet, unaccountably she was afraid, poised for flight if only she dared. Her feelings tumbled through consciousness, robbing her of rational thought.

He reached out and closed his arms around her, resting his hands against her spine. She had longed and longed for this moment, desired to feel his assertion of physical control over her, yearned for the licence to touch him. Yet suddenly she was seized with a terrible emptiness and a bleak despair at her inability to respond to him. As his lips rested on hers she tried most urgently to feel something — but there was nothing at all, just the sensation of pressure on her mouth. Her eyes were closed tightly as though to shut him out. She could not understand what was happening to her. She rested limply in his arms.

He kissed expertly, holding her face in his hands with a certain skill as though calculating in what way he might best arouse her. He pushed the hardness of his body against her so that she could feel the taut muscles of his thighs. But her genuine attempts to respond failed miserably. She was like a child disappointed with a present that had been lingeringly anticipated over many weeks; it was not possible to conceal the anti-climax.

She felt his arms stiffen and then drop away from her, opened her eyes to see his face angered and shamed, heard his voice lash out into the muffled stillness: 'So, after those pretty girlish blushes, you're a cool little customer underneath it all, are you?'

'Oh, Phillippe.' She felt she had given him a dreadful rebuke. 'I'm sorry,' she whispered.

The harsh glinting flash from his eye suggested that she had said quite the wrong thing. He was not a man who wanted pity.

'No need,' he said coldly. 'I'm sorry if I offended you. I should know by now not to mix business with pleasure.' He brushed a speck of fluff from his sleeve. 'Make sure the horse is cooled off before you rug her up,' he said curtly. 'We don't want any mishaps among the top ranks, do we — either human or equine.' He looked at his watch. It was obvious he had no intention of prolonging matters. 'I'm rather late for an engagement,' he said abruptly. 'Goodnight.'

He walked away casually as though nothing unusual had happened. She stared in astonishment, feeling that he had revolutionised her world in a matter of seconds.

She put the horse away with mechanical efficiency and ran to the cottage as though it were a haven. She switched on the television — in need of its capacity to blot out personal sensations. As the picture swam on to the screen she moved about busily, trying to keep herself occupied. She came upon her reflection in the pine-framed mirror over the desk — white face, large eyes puzzled and wounded, lips pale — pale and chastised-looking. His touch had in some way left them feeling cheated and punished. She moved her fingers over the soft roundness in bewilderment.

Around eleven she went to bed and fell asleep instantly. But later in the night she was restless, hovering on the line dividing consciousness from sleep. The feel of strange hands roving over her body, touching the secret sensitive places where only one special person should be allowed, troubled her. She turned from side to side in agitation and it was almost dawn when she slipped again into sleep.

Just before waking, her half-consciousness still clouded by dreams, she experienced a deep sensation of safety, warmth and protection. She was surrounded with intangible peacefulness. She was talking, shaking out her thoughts without fear or hesitation and they were being listened to with care, considered with gentle justice. She was striving to get nearer to the source of warmth but it eluded her; her body felt slow and heavy and she could not move. She woke suddenly, and lay motionless, still under the influence of the sensations that had spilled out from unconsciousness. As the drowsiness slipped from her so did the feelings of security and shelter. She tried in vain to recapture them but they had vanished into the inaccessible areas of her mind.

She got up and dressed quickly in jeans and a warm sweater. An icy cold hung around the upstairs rooms of the cottage. She scraped away the ashes from the open fireplace and lit some fresh logs. She made coffee and took a cup up to Vinnie who lay sleeping like an infant, her hair ruffled out on the pillow in russet-coloured abundance.

After a light breakfast she went out into the stable yard to attend to her horses. The harsh reality of the day was asserting itself — the real world where dependence could only be on herself. But the sensations of her drowsy state refused to be completely shaken off. As she worked briskly over the Princess's flanks with her brush the assortment of feelings and images suddenly assembled themselves into a recognisable shape — a known form with human substance.

She paused and leaned heavily in shock against the door of the horse's box. Max Thornton's face filled her imagination and swept away all other images. She gasped out loud, amazed at her own blindness. It's Max I love, she said to herself, not Phillippe at all. She had mistaken her ease in his presence as a mark of impartiality, her trust as a sign of emotional neutrality. Well, of course, Phillippe was desperately attractive, there was no denying it, but he was restless and moody, self-centred and insecure. He was still growing up, she thought indulgently, inclined to feel very forgiving.

On the crest of an emotional wave,

she almost ran back to the cottage to share her discovery with Vinnie! An internal warning note sounded and with solemn deliberation she set to work again. Doubts began to take hold of her. What did Max really think of her? He seemed to regard her very highly — but did it mean anything? She could not help going over what Vinnie had said about him. Eventually she put it all out of her mind. She would just leave things to time and fate. It would surely turn out satisfactorily.

★   ★   ★

Despite Vinnie's teasing and supposed help Janet managed to be dressed and ready for Max's arrival by 6.45.

'You look absolutely edible, darling,' Vinnie said smugly, 'he simply will not be able to resist you.'

Janet was startled at her appearance in the expensive clothes Vinnie had loaned. They gave her an air of polish and sophistication she had not associated with herself before. She had washed her hair and blow-dried it into a swooping curve around her face — 'lovely, pet,' was Vinnie's verdict, 'just like an upturned daffodil!' Vinnie drenched her in Dior eau de toilette and pronounced her well and truly ready. 'I wonder what *he'll* be wearing,' she said in her wickedest drawl. 'Will it be the wildly elegant dark suit with the manly wrist flashing sexily from the snow-white cuff — or the country casuals elegance — all cuddly in tantalisingly tickly tweed?'

'Time alone will tell,' Janet said, hoping her feelings were not showing through any slight cracks in her rigidly maintained self-composure.

'Do you think he'll bring a gift?' Vinnie said, 'like old-fashioned heroes in novels, a profusion of roses resting in acres of white tissue, or a box of chocolates girded with a pink satin ribbon?'

'I hate chocolates,' Janet said lightly.

Vinnie sighed. 'Hmm — well *you've* only your little self to give him!' she concluded, 'but that's plenty. *I've* never *seen* you look so gorgeous. I'd like to wrap you up in a parcel and send it to him with a handle frequently label stuck on the front.'

Janet laughed and tried to ignore the rush of warmth to her cheeks at Vinnie's words.

They heard the noise of a car. Vinnie consulted her watch as a sweep of headlights swung around the corner of the courtyard. 'What you might call punctual,' she said, grinning.

Janet was almost sick with anticipation. She looked for a brief, anxious moment at Vinnie.

'I'm not coming down,' Vinnie said quietly, 'he's to be all yours tonight, pet.' She bent and gave her friend a light kiss, then made her way to the bathroom, dropping her satin négligée down from one shoulder and turning back with a seductive wink.

Max was already on the doorstep.

When she opened the door, he smiled at her as he always did in his gentle, honest way. 'Hullo!' he said — 'is the ankle better. Are you all in one piece?'

She smiled back and momentarily closed her eyes in relief. There had been no need to feel nervous. He was just as he always was; why hadn't she had the sense to think of that through the last few tense hours.

The car standing under the cottage windows was low and white with a huge elongated bonnet and shiny wire wheels. It was certainly not the Rover. She sank down into it as he held the door for her and watched with interest as he folded his long frame almost in two to get into the driver's seat.

The engine growled like a velvet-throated tiger when he turned the key and a burst of music came from the stereo cassette. He reached over quickly and turned a switch. The music vanished.

'Sorry,' he said, 'I'm afraid I overdo the loud pedal when I'm on my own.'

'It's all right,' she said a little stiffly — 'I don't mind listening.'

He smiled and glanced at her. 'Oh, no,' he said significantly, 'I can listen to my tapes any time.'

He drove the car carefully over the bumpy lane and then accelerated hard into the road beyond.

'Well!' he said, 'aren't you going to talk to me?'

'I'm a bit lost for words,' she said. 'This car . . . '

'Yes?'

'Well — I like it,' she said at last.

'Thank you, so do I,' he replied drily.

Yet somehow, she thought, it did not quite fit with him. She frowned trying to work out why not.

'What's the matter?' he asked.

She was startled. He had not been looking at her. How had he sensed her puzzlement?

She hesitated, with anyone else she would have brushed the question aside, turned lightly to another topic. But with Max she felt the freedom to say anything she liked.

'The car,' she said — 'it isn't what I expected!'

He laughed. He had a wonderfully joyful laugh, completely infectious.

'Go on,' he instructed. 'I'm intrigued.'

'Well,' she floundered, 'I didn't know you had another car and this one . . . ' she was not quite sure how to express her thoughts.

'It doesn't suit my image,' he suggested helpfully.

'Yes.'

'Or rather,' he went on, 'it doesn't suit the image you have of me!'

'Oh dear, you're losing me,' she said.

'No, it's quite simple; we all have different pictures and ideas of different people and of ourselves as well. I suppose that's what is meant by the individual point of view.'

Yes, he was right, of course, although she had never thought it out so clearly herself.

'Anyway,' he went on, 'about the car.

I suspect that in your mind you have a picture of the sort of man who might drive a fifteen-year-old E-type Jaguar that's something of a collector's piece!'

Yes, she thought, conjuring up an olive-skinned young man with black hair and handsomely cruel features.

He was laughing again. 'Well, I don't know what you're thinking,' he said, 'but if you were to start actually looking you'd find that there wasn't a 'type'. All kinds of people drive them, just like all kinds of people go to cricket matches or read Shakespeare — or ride horses,' he added pointedly, turning briefly to smile at her.

She reflected on what he had said. He talked to her differently from anyone she had known before. He gave her interesting things to think about — it even took her mind off the fact that she was quite madly in love with him.

'Janet,' he said, pulling her out of her thoughts, 'have you ever bought yourself a present because you wanted to celebrate some private happiness — or perhaps because you wanted to comfort yourself when you were feeling miserable?'

She considered. Yes, she had, she supposed most people had at some time.

'And usually it's something rather selfish; extravagant perhaps?'

She grinned in agreement.

'Well,' he said, patting the dashboard, 'there you are then!'

She wondered whether the purchase had been prompted by happiness or misery. She knew he would tell her if she asked but she felt it would be intruding on his privacy. She glanced at his face; there was no need to ask. The pain was clearly visible. She could not bear to think of running the risk of hurting him by opening up the wounds. She longed to wrap her arms around him and stroke the hurt from his face. She relaxed into the firm warmth of the leather seats and abandoned herself to the unconflicted enjoyment of his presence, the intimacy of being alone with him in the stillness of the countryside as the car cut through the blackness — a shell of white steel binding them together, shutting all the rest of the world out. He drove with considerable skill, using the car's power to the full, accelerating through the corners so that it clung to the road as though fastened with invisible wires.

★   ★   ★

The cathedral was filling up with people when they arrived. It was a small but splendid building standing in a solid and protective manner on the east side of an old market town. People had come from miles around to attend the concert, from the outlying villages to the north and from the cities to the south. The women's clothes formed a brilliant mosaic against the sombre background of the men's dark suits and the cathedral's grey stone and carved oak. It was as though a flock of butterflies had filled the air on a rain-soaked afternoon.

Janet was not at all surprised to find that Max was a perfect escort. He had the knack of being on hand to guide and help without seeming to fuss or becoming impatient.

They found their seats and settled down, commenting to each other on their luck in having an excellent view of the orchestra. Most of the players were assembled, plucking and blowing experimentally. Janet caught the air of excitement as little trills from a flute rose up into the high-vaulted roof to merge with the deep urgent throbbing of the bass drum. She turned impulsively to Max. He was already watching her. He raised his eyebrows questioningly.

'I feel so happy,' she said without warning. Her heart turned over as he gave one of his gentle searching smiles. He leaned slightly towards her and for a moment she thought that he was going to kiss her, kiss her full on the lips, right there in front of all those people. Instead he said lightly — 'I hope it's going to live up to your expectation.'

The conductor appeared, a hush fell and then suddenly the building was filled with sound. It was the most triumphant and sparkling sound, suffused with all the shades of feeling Janet associated with youthfulness and well-being. She could feel it gliding and dipping inside her, in hundreds of small springs of gladness. She could hardly contain herself from saying something out loud — joining in the creation of this intense pleasure. She looked around. People appeared unmoved, solemn and thoughtful. She turned to Max in surprise. His eyes were crinkled in amusement; he winked at her in a leisurely fashion, making her want to laugh.

At the end of the piece she threw herself into a frenzy of excited clapping.

Max grinned and said, 'Pull yourself together.'

'That was wonderful,' she exclaimed. 'What was it?'

'Bach,' he said. 'I wish he could have been here to see you, I think he might have been rather gratified.'

She hesitated. 'I know hardly anything about music,' she said. 'I've never been to a concert like this before.'

'Music is like good food,' he said, 'you don't have to know anything about it to enjoy it.'

But the next piece was very dreary, a lament, formless and uninspiring. She diverted her attention to her companion, sliding her eyes towards him without appearing to stare. He was gazing ahead, his features tranquil and grave. She wondered why she had not realised before how splendid he was. Perhaps because he was not handsome in a conventional, showy way like Phillippe but rather had a strength and definition of feature that one had to become familiar with to appreciate fully. She noticed two little grooves running in a bow shape around the corners of his mouth. They were lines telling of countless laughs and smiles, gentle, ironic, teasing, warm, rueful, sarcastic, puzzled. She wished she could lay her lips on them and trace their course with the tip of her tongue. His hands, lying loosely clasped on his knee, were large and resolute, the fingers long and solid with white-rimmed nails. She remembered the reassurance of their firmness on her skin. She guessed that he must be tremendously strong with those massive shoulders and long legs. But he seemed unaware of his body; its energy and power were held in reserve — quiet and restrained — like his cars, she decided, smiling at the neat comparison.

A tremor of intense longing reached down inside her. He was a gem, a hard, glowing sapphire, brilliant and strong with a soft warm light in its heart. She wanted him. Yet only hours ago she had thought she wanted Phillippe; she felt hot with the humiliation of it.

There was Mozart to finish with.

'He'll make a good pudding!' Max said, with a rueful smile. 'I'm afraid the main course was a bit indigestible.'

The Mozart was all lightness and delicacy, with a wistfulness behind it which gave it a quality of haunting beauty. Janet was unaccountably reminded of Brio — of his elegant, precise movements and the knowing but faintly wounded expression in his dark eyes. But this was not a time to worry about Brio, there were other issues to be considered.

The evening was racing on, tumbling away like the hours of a child's birthday. She tried to concentrate on each minute and imprison it within her grasp.

The crowd thronged out into the cold air when the final applause had subsided. Janet felt she was going to be lost in the crush but Max took her hand and held her tightly until they reached the car. She shivered against the leather which had cooled to match the atmosphere. He switched the heater on at full and told her off for not bringing a coat.

She held her breath, wondering if he planned to take her straight back to the cottage. She remembered Vinnie's chiding remarks about her waiting around for Phillippe to snap his fingers. Was she doing the same with Max? Surely there was no need; if she wanted his company for longer all she had to do was tell him. She opened her mouth but no words came. He said, 'Are you hungry?'

She laughed in surprise; she hadn't thought about it — but, yes she was hungry.

'How about supper at the Thornlea?' he asked, raising her spirits at a stroke. 'The restaurant's closed and empty — but the fridge should be full. We can choose what we like.'

'Yes, please!' she said. She stretched her legs out and closed her eyes. 'Oh, Max,' she said with a sighing laugh, 'this is a lovely evening!'

She waited for one of his dry comments but he said nothing, he must be concentrating on his driving. The road was dark and curvy and they were doing 65.

'You like driving, don't you?' she said.

'Yes — I do. Can you drive?'

'Yes.' Harry had paid for lessons and she had recently passed her test. He began to slow down. 'Would you like to drive now?'

'Oh no!'

'Why not?'

'Well, I'm not very experienced.'

'There's only one way to remedy that, isn't there?' he said.

The car was already stationary. She was enormously tempted but a little afraid. 'All right,' she said. They changed places, he adjusted the seat for her, showed her the controls. She set off gingerly but soon her confidence grew as she discovered the car's good-mannered restraint. It seemed perfectly at ease doing 45 and Max also was totally relaxed, humming a tune and tapping his fingers on his knee.

'Shall we have some music?' he asked. He switched on the tape. There was a wonderful feeling of closeness with him, and joy in sharing the delicate cascade of musical notes.

They were well into the country now, about three miles from the Thornlea. The road was established and elderly, used to carrying one car at a time but quite prepared to accommodate two if need be — providing they both proceeded with care. Its dips and climbs presented little challenge for the car, which pulled eagerly up the slopes yet was quickly responsive to a gentle checking back as it topped each summit and tried to roll away unhampered through the descent beyond. It was a delight to drive.

Janet saw the lights of another car, swaying in the distance. With a shock she realised that they were approaching very fast, reeling and plunging, disappearing momentarily as the road sank down leaving a chasm of blackness and giving a short respite during which anxiety took firm root. A gentle rocking halo of silver fuzz preceeded the full final dazzle as the lights swooped over the curve of the road with dizzy brilliance. The glare seemed crazily uncontrolled. She was painfully alert behind the wheel, conscious of her total responsibility to salvage something from this menace whose advent had been so incredibly swift and unexpected.

The lights seemed about to pierce them and then miraculously they were gone and the Jaguar was resting on soft ground, slightly tilted, with its headlights tracing the shiny knots of a tree behind the hedge. The nerves in her arms and legs were twitching fiercely. Her throat was dry.

'Fool!' Max said violently. She had never heard him angry before. She knew the word was meant for the driver of the departing car. It sliced through the air to cut and jar as though his fury was all for her.

She was drenched in helpless shame.

If only she could turn the clock back thirty seconds. If only she had not agreed to drive.

'Well,' he said, quite mildly, 'we'd better get out and have a look.'

# 9

The rear end of the car was nudged down into the grass, its nearside wheel perched on the edge of a narrow ditch. The actual damage seemed slight. Probably no more than a slight buckle under the bumper. Max judged that they had had a miraculous escape. He examined the car's position, wondering what was the best thing to do. Janet stood nearby, silent and shivering.

'Is it badly damaged?' she said at last.

'No,' he said, 'it's getting it back on the road again that's going to be the problem.'

'Oh, I'm sorry.' Her voice was miserable and resigned. She kicked nervously at tufts of grass.

'Right then,' he was saying in his kind, even voice. 'You get in and put it into first gear — I'll push and we'll see if we can get it on four wheels again.

Plenty of revs but don't let the clutch out too quickly.'

She held on hard to stop herself bursting into a storm of frustrated tears. 'I don't want to drive any more,' she said, walking away from him, her feet squeaking on the wet grass.

His voice came through the darkness — amused rather than exasperated. 'Janet?' he asked patiently, 'how tall would you say I am?'

She ignored his question.

'Look,' he said, the amusement all evaporated, 'you may be as strong as an ox but I'm going to have all on to shift it with my twelve stone, so I don't think you are going to do much better. You drive and I'll push.'

Impasse! The tension between them was as taut and fine as a silken rope.

'I don't want to drive,' she repeated, knowing it was mulish but unable to stop herself. 'And I wish you hadn't asked me to in the first place,' she cried savagely. She could feel her eyes blazing into the darkness.

There was a moment of suspense, then suddenly he sprang at her, gripping her shoulders. 'For God's sake just get in and drive it, Janet!' he shouted.

She said nothing, she stood passive and inactive under his grasp. She tried to wriggle away but he was shaking her, pushing and pulling her shoulders rhythmically with his hands. She began to struggle — not in fear, but in an effort to assert herself. Still he went on in rigid three time, one two three, one two three. Shaking and shaking. She could feel the power in his arms, feel the force oozing from his fingertips. A desperate and terrible anger was struggling to free itself from him.

In time his grip slackened and he staggered against her as though relieved. He was moaning softly against her neck. She put her hands up behind his head. Then without any preliminaries he was clutching her to him, pressing his lips against hers with breathtaking urgency. She collapsed against him drinking him in, pushing her tongue up between his teeth. Delicious waves of pain flowed through her body like sweeps of moving sunlight across a hillside. She seemed to be opening up inside like a flower, a tender warm wound, longing to receive him. The desire reached down into her flanks, spreading through her hips and thighs so that she was gasping aloud with pleasure, with the ecstasy of wanting him. She had her arms around him under his jacket, fierce and protecting. He no longer seemed split off from her — they were both parts of the darkness. There was nothing but him in her heart and mind for those few moments.

When his hands, wild and hungry, touched the rounded warmth of the skin under her blouse he was suddenly pulled up — brought to a screeching halt. 'Oh God,' he groaned from deep inside. 'What am I doing?'

She dropped away quietly from him

and smiled. Suddenly she saw things differently. His feelings for her were quite obvious. He could not possibly kiss and caress her like that unless he loved her. She was filled with a wonderful sense of power. She could do anything now, anything at all. Drive the car out of a six-foot snow drift if necessary.

'I'll have a try,' she said cheerfully. 'Plenty of revs — first gear . . . '

Max put his hands against the cold white steel. For a few seconds the spinning, futile wheel decorated him with a stream of mud and then, miraculously, the wheel lifted and the car bumped softly on to the verge.

'Done it,' he called triumphantly. Flicking mud from his thick cord jacket, he strode round to the car door and started to edge into the passenger seat.

She moved as though to get out and let him drive. 'No — you drive,' he commanded.

'Oh, Max, Please!'

'Come on! We've been through all this before.'

'I'm surprised you have any confidence in me.'

'On the contrary, if your reactions had not been so swift we might both be dead.'

She was doubtful. 'I've lost a bit of confidence myself.'

'I thought so. That's why you must drive. You always get back on a horse when you've fallen off, don't you — so as not to lose nerve?'

'Yes.'

'Well then?'

'Oh, I suppose you're right.'

'Of course I am. Come on, get on with it.'

His good humour seemed completely recovered. They reached the Thornlea at midnight and Janet was already beginning to wonder if the last hour had any reality to it. She determined not to ignore the recent episode — she must find out what had lain behind Max's anger and then they must affirm their love for each other.

Max took her on a brief tour of the kitchens at the Thornlea. She found it hard to imagine that food was prepared there, they were so immaculate.

'Come and see the wine; that's far more interesting,' he said.

In the cellars the wine bottles lay in rows, their smooth bulges covered with dust and the flecked plaster that fell from the whitewashed ceilings. They seemed to be silent and waiting, full of the promise of dreams, elation, oblivion — sorrow perhaps.

'This is the really good stuff here,' Max said. 'The table wines are next door.' He looked along the shelves, considering the bottles, before reaching up and grasping one with a thick, wired neck.

'Champagne!' he said. 'I seem to remember that you enjoy that. We'll have a glass to warm ourselves up.'

He took her back through the restaurant and up the stairs to his own suite of rooms.

'I remember coming up here!' Janet said ruefully.

'You do?' was his dry comment. 'I rather doubted that you were fully conscious.'

The room in which he read, listened to music and relaxed seemed to merit the title of a drawing room, Janet thought. It was long and gracious; more beautiful and imaginatively arranged than any other room she had been in. There was the soft gleam of brass and the sheen of leather upholstery. Abundant plants in porcelain pots threw magical reflections on the plain white walls. A low fire was smouldering in the open grate. Max tossed some logs on to it, bringing it to life with a flurry of orange sparks.

'Are you still hungry?' he asked, 'after those adventures?'

She gazed up at him, trying to read his thoughts, but for once his face gave nothing away.

'Not very,' she said uncertainly. He regarded her thoughtfully.

'I'll just get you something,' he said. 'I won't be long.'

After a few moments she became restless and went to join him in the kitchen. He was slicing a delicious smelling cylindrical lump of beef, crusty on the outside and pink in the middle. He was both swift and skilful.

'Gosh!' she said in admiration.

'Max the knife,' he said, laughing at her and brandishing the thin blade.

She felt that his good-humoured cheerfulness was in some way keeping her at bay. She was absolutely determined not to fall into the role of the helpless bystander with Max as she had with Phillippe. Her feeling of ease in being able to communicate with him was one of the reasons why she loved him so much. She could not let him withdraw from her and hide within himself.

The bottle gave a muffled 'thlup' sound as he eased the cork from its neck. He gave her a tulip-shaped glass of the sparkling liquid which seemed almost to be alive, dancing under her nose in a shower of cold pricks.

'Cheers!' he said, smiling.

She touched his arm lightly, although she would rather have slid her arm around him, put her body close to his to comfort him, for she sensed that that was what he needed.

'Max?' she said gently, 'what was it all about?'

He looked down steadily at her. 'I was going to tell you,' he said softly. 'I was just wondering how to say it.'

He hooked one of his long legs over the table and rested his weight on it. He looked at her in his open, tender way. She felt as though warm liquid were being poured through her body, making her almost stagger with the burden of wanting him.

'Janet,' he said, in a soft, caressing voice, 'you're such a nice person.' A sudden chill struck in her heart at those words; they did not seem like a prelude to a declaration of love. Confidence began to ooze out of her.

'I wanted your friendship and companionship,' he told her gently. 'I wanted it very much — but that seems so difficult to achieve between a man and a woman, doesn't it? Especially as I'm older and established and you're very young and just starting out.'

'Yes,' she said, trying hard to sound bright and sensible, 'I know.'

'I suppose I just wasn't prepared for my own feelings,' he said enigmatically. He propelled her through into the drawing room, indicating that she should sit by the fire. It seemed that he sas saying, 'Are you sitting comfortably, then I'll begin.' There was going to be a long story.

'I came here three years ago,' he said. 'The house was in a bad state. It was damp, neglected and generally rather sad. It belonged to an aunt of mine. I remember it as it was when I was a kid, full of lights and log fires and a huge glittering tree at Christmas time. My aunt had two daughters, around my age. When they were students, my uncle killed himself and them driving back from a New Year's party. My aunt survived but she was never the same. She insisted on living in the house all alone — and she let it disintegrate around her! No one in the family could do a thing about it. She fell out with my parents, never saw them for years until my father died. For some reason my aunt — Ann, she was called — had always had a fondness for me — and I for her as well. That did not stop me being amazed that when she died she left me the house and quite a few thousand pounds.' He stopped and gave his listener a quizzical look.

'Am I boring you?' he asked softly.

Janet shook her head.

'I was practising as a lawyer at the time. I'd never really wanted to do that job — I just ended up doing it because it was what my parents had wanted. Anyway I had begun to dislike it — quite intensely in fact, so I took the opportunity to give it up and start something here.'

'Goodness!' Janet said. 'Just like that!'

'Ah, well, I did get a little help.'

She caught her breath. She suspected that a blow was going to fall. It did.

'I was engaged to a girl at the time. Her father had — still has — a chain of wine bars here in the North. With her encouragement, his contacts and my new riches I managed to get something going here in the food and drink line. The first year was absolute hell — and profitless, but then things picked up. And now . . . ' he raised his hands in a movement of humorous amazement — 'Well — I don't seem to be able to go wrong — at least in business, that is,' he added significantly.

They sat quietly for a while sipping the champagne.

'Tell me about your fiancée,' Janet said, running a finger around the top of her glass until it squeaked in protest.

He got up and opened a drawer in the mahogany desk opposite the fire-place. He handed her a photograph. It showed a young woman, beautiful, poised and exquisitely dressed in unmistakably expensive casualness. She was a silky-haired blonde with high, rounded cheek bones and splendid deep-lidded eyes. Her mouth was large and curved. Janet imagined Max's lips searching for its soft warmth and a dark chill settled inside her.

'Oh — she's lovely!' she said, her voice brittle with forced enthusiasm.

'Yes!' Max agreed, his voice dry and emotionless.

'She was a very ambitious girl, also a lawyer. About a couple of years ago she was invited to take part in a TV programme about the legal aspects of women's rights.' He grinned, his brown eyes crinkling with genuine amusement. 'She went down rather well as you might guess. In fact she was a wow. She was soon broadcasting regularly on women's programmes — always on the women's rights angle. She became something of a national expert.'

Janet picked up the photograph again

and studied it. 'I've seen her on TV, haven't it?' she asked. 'It's Jane Denver.'

'That's right!'

'Goodness,' she exclaimed, judging that the glamorous and ruthlessly clever Jane must have been quite a handful. 'What happened then?' she asked.

'She was in London more and more and the question of marriage seemed to retreat into a hazy sometime, maybe never, sort of idea.'

'Oh, poor Max,' she said in swift sympathy, 'were you sad about it?'

His eyes travelled solemnly across her face. She felt the question to be embarrassingly naïve. A flush sprang to her cheeks.

'What a kind girl you are,' he said softly, sending knives turning in her heart at the thought of all his tenderness, which seemed to be slipping from her grasp.

'Yes, I was sad. Angry as well. She was very keen on being independent and I was more than encouraging on that score. I had no wish to tie her down even though I wanted to marry her. I was quite prepared for her to have her profession, a flat in London and so on. I thought it would raise problems, but not insurmountable ones!'

How could anyone not marry him, Janet thought. He's so gentle and considerate and wonderful. Tears stung the back of her eyelids at the injustice of it all.

He gazed thoughtfully into the fire. A shower of sparks clung in trembling brilliance to the sooty inside of the chimney.

'Did she leave you for her career?' Janet suggested timidly, desperate to know what the situation was now.

He sighed.

'No,' he said. 'That's the irony of it. She left me to get married to an excessively rich banker, threw up her job and settled into the role of full-time wife and society hostess. It's funny,' he added, 'how people are so blind about what they really want.'

'I'm sorry,' Janet said.

He looked gravely at her. 'So am I,' he said quietly, 'especially for all that . . . anger you received tonight. You didn't deserve it.'

No, thought Janet. It wasn't for me, any of it, the anger or the passion. It was all for someone else. He just wanted her for a friend; he thought she loved Phillippe.

He was regarding her with a worried expression. 'Do you forgive me?' he said urgently.

'Yes.' She heard her voice as though it were coming from far away, resigned and lifeless. She felt crushed and unbearably weary.

'Will you take me home, Max, please,' she said, getting up to fetch the Paisley shawl, feeling a terrible dreadness in her limbs as she walked.

'Of course!' He jumped up, then he put out a hand towards her, but she could take no more. She shook her head and gestured him gently away.

In the car they were quiet and polite. Janet felt as though happiness were draining slowly out of her, never to return. It seemed there was nothing but misery stretching on ahead, day after day, week after week. She did not know how she would bear it.

# 10

Her mother met her at the station in her bright, new, red Mini-Metro.

'Are you all right, dear?' she said anxiously, stamping warm damp kisses on her face.

'Yes!' Janet was able to sound reassuring. 'I just felt so tired. I had to have a break.'

'Oh, I get so worried,' her mother said, eyeing her with the sureness of an expert — taking in all the danger signs: loss of weight, pallor, slatey smudges under the eyes.

'Now tell me if you're not warm enough, love,' she said as she groped in her bag for the ignition keys. 'I can get the motor rug out of the boot.'

Janet laughed. 'I'm not ill, Mum,' she said. 'Come on, get this super car started — I'm dying to get home.'

'Oh,' her mother said, 'isn't it a lovely

little car. Harry just brought it home one day. He gave me a big bunch of flowers with a key tucked inside and said, 'Go and see if it fits the car in the drive! Can you believe it?'

'Lovely!' said Janet, referring to both the car and Harry's romantic gesture. Her mother's girlish, starry-eyed happiness made her feel about a hundred.

In the evening Harry insisted on taking 'my two girls' out to dinner. Janet felt it was important to make an effort to look nice, but even five days after her evening with Max her limbs still felt leaden and disobedient. It seemed to take her ages to do anything at all. She spent long periods just standing lost in thought. This evening she had to force herself to choose some clothes to wear and it was only with an enormous effort that she got herself dressed and made up.

'You look lovely, dear!' her mother said, as they waited for Harry to bring his car around to the front gate.

'Now!' Harry said with amiable

joviality, as he parked the car outside the restaurant, 'aren't I lucky, with two beautiful girls to escort?'

Janet tried hard to smile. She kept on smiling and smiling, feeling as though the expression were fixed on with glue and tacks.

The restaurant was hushed and a little gloomy in Janet's opinion. It was the most renowned and expensive one in the district and to eat there was something of a luxury. But compared with the Thornlea it was dreary and lifeless. The food was too elaborate, the service too formal, the whole place lacking the imaginative touch of someone who had a finger on everything that went on, who knew just what was required to make the customers fully at ease and happy.

Her aching loneliness for Max filled her up entirely. There was a sensation of despair and loss as grim and dark as grief for a dead loved one. She had fought it fiercely all week. Yet strangely her professional life had remained unaffected. If anything her riding had improved. Even Phillippe had been moved to give a little cool praise. He was obviously still smarting from her rejection but it did not disturb her. She suddenly found that she could handle him with superb ease. Phillippe was not going to pose any problem at all.

I can do without you, Max Thornton, she kept telling herself but occasionally a wild and terrible longing for his presence, the sound of his voice, the sight of his face, burst through her self-control, leaving her weak and demoralised. She knew that she must have familiar loving faces to support her; that was why she had decided to come home for a few days.

Whether home made things easier seemed doubtful. Her mother was still behaving like an ecstatic bride and Harry carried on like some lovable, balding Prince Charming. Janet felt as though she were positioned at the furthest point in an elongated triangle.

'It's a beautiful meal,' she told Harry

as she pushed some creamed salmon around her plate, hoping that it would disappear without her having to make the effort of chewing or swallowing it.

'I somehow don't think you're at your best to enjoy it,' he said slowly, giving her a questioningly perceptive look. Janet was coming to realise why her mother was so unshamedly in love with him. He had the same quiet thoughtfulness which so endeared her to Max. She felt that both Harry and her mother deserved her honesty.

'No,' she said, 'you're right.'

'What is it, dear?' her mother said anxiously.

Janet shrugged. 'Oh,' she said with a rueful smile, 'unlucky in love I suppose.'

She noticed her mother's hand creep towards Harry's over the tablecloth.

'Unlike you two!' she added with a grin.

'Oh dear.' Her mother was immediately stricken with guilt at being happy in the face of her daughter's obvious misery. 'Now what did you say he was called, this young man — Phillippe — that's it, isn't it?'

Janet paused.

Her mother pinkened. 'Oh dear, have I got the wrong name?'

Janet could not avoid laughing.

'Is it someone else?' Harry asked gravely.

'Yes,' Janet smiled gratefully at her stepfather. He was certainly good at inspiring confidence.

'He's called Max Thornton,' she said, feeling a slight shiver of pleasure just to be able to say his name out loud in someone else's presence.

'What does he do, dear?' her mother asked, getting down to the essentials without delay.

'He owns and runs a restaurant.'

Her mother started. 'Like this one?' she whispered, a gleam of speculation flickering in her eyes.

'Even better,' Janet whispered back, a little mischievously.

'Oh!' Her mother retired into a

slightly stunned silence.

'And what of his character?' Harry asked with a considerate pomposity that made Janet want to laugh.

'Do you mean are his intentions honourable?' Janet asked, still a little hesitant about describing Max seriously in case it became too painful.

'Janet!' her mother said.

'Don't worry, Mum, he's very honourable,' she said, reflecting that perhaps it would be better if Max were less highly principled. 'And he's kind and gentle and full of fun and he makes you feel special and important,' she said, surprised to hear the words tumble out.

Harry said gravely, 'You love him, don't you?'

She nodded, looking down at her plate where the food lay in a congealed pinkish mess. Her stomach twisted in revulsion. She imagined Max coming to pick her up from home, taking her back to the Thornlea, tempting her with some delicious food he had prepared

246

himself, taking her to bed and making love to her with lingering tenderness.

'What are you smiling at, dear?' her mother said innocently.

'Oh now, Mary,' Harry interposed, 'isn't it obvious. When you're in love you have very smiling kind of thoughts.'

Janet felt a throbbing of blood in her cheeks. Had Harry guessed what she was thinking? She supposed he had. After all he and her mother were newly weds. Just because they were middle-aged did not mean they did not have desires as desperate and pervasive as hers.

'So, we've heard all good things up until now, Janet. What is the problem?' Harry asked.

She thought about it. She had thought about it a good deal previously. The conclusion was an especially bleak one.

'He doesn't love me!' she said simply. 'He just thinks of me as a friend.'

'Ah,' said Harry, pausing as a girl came to bring the pudding, 'but surely that's the best way to start?'

Janet agreed, half-heartedly. It seemed to her that things were all finished with Max — not starting at all.

Her mother was staring worriedly at her daughter.

'I can't get used to it, dear,' she said helplessly. 'I'd been thinking about this young man Phillippe and now I have to think about someone called Max.'

Harry shot a glance at her. It was a definite warning not to go too far.

Harry looked thoughtful, attacked his pudding and without warning launched into an amusing account of an especially difficult incident in school which had taken a lot of sorting out. The conversation having drifted on to school matters then stayed in that area and both Max and Phillippe faded out of the limelight leaving Janet feeling strangely relieved.

It was late when they arrived home and Janet went straight to bed, but was not at all surprised to hear her mother's hesitant tap on the door as she lay trying to sleep.

'I know you're tired, dear, but you'll have to tell me all about it. I shan't be able to sleep a wink otherwise!'

Janet reached out and took her mother's hand and squeezed it hard. She told her about Phillippe, how she had once felt about him, how it all seemed so strange now because she just regarded him with a certain kind of friendly sympathy. She told her about Max, how she had met him, the evening at Alexa's house, the night of the concert. But she said nothing about the sudden dark and angry embrace, the crushing strength of Max's arms and his powerful body, pressed hard against hers, as though he would break down all the barriers between them, fuse them together as though they were one. That was her secret, too exquisitely painful and precious to be shared with anyone.

'So,' she concluded, amazed at her composure, 'I shall just have to be content to think of him as a friend.'

'Oh dear,' her mother said, her eyes tragically large with sympathy. 'Is he very rich, Janet?' she asked abruptly, creating a change of mood.

Janet had never consciously asked herself whether Max was rich. The fact that he had a big house, a successful business, two cars and a wardrobe full of suits she had taken for granted as being a part of his personality and lifestyle. She gave a wistful smile and told her mother that she supposed he was rich.

Her mother sighed and received a gently disapproving prod from her daughter.

'Mercenary!' Janet whispered.

'No, dear, just wanting the very best for you — in every way,' her mother said sadly before creeping back to her waiting husband.

Janet found sleep evasive after six in the morning. She got up and padded around in the kitchen, putting on the kettle to make tea to take up to her mother and Harry. But Harry came down before the tea was ready, ruffled and warm with sleep, looking like some balding teddy bear.

He sat down at the kitchen table and watched Janet pour boiling water into the teapot. Then he made her heart thunder as he said, 'This man you told us about — Max — you said he was kind?'

'Oh, yes.' The warmth in her voice was immediately flaming in her cheeks.

'Mmm, that's good.' Harry was a deliberate and composed sitting there in his pyjamas as though he were behind his large desk at school. 'And is he good enough for you?' he continued.

Janet stared at him and frowned a little. 'Yes . . . yes, I think he is.'

'I'm being quite serious, Janet. It's an old cliché but it means something. You can be infatuated with someone and it blinds you to all the negative points in their personality. You're a special person, you need someone equally special.'

'Oh, Harry,' she burst out, 'you are good, you do seem to understand . . . '

'And how old is he?' Harry continued, unmoved by his step-daughter's sudden rush of feeling.

'I don't know — thirty or thirty-five, perhaps. Does it matter?'

'No, it doesn't matter, but it makes a difference.' After some moments of reflection he said, 'So; we have a well-set-up, successful, cultured, sensitive and kind man in his thirties with an unhappy love affair behind him.'

'Yes,' said Janet, impressed at this accurate portrait.

'Seems too good to miss,' Harry murmured. 'I'm going to offer some advice now,' he said. 'I'm not asking whether you want it or expecting you to accept it, but I'm going to give it anyway.'

'Yes,' she said patiently, smiling at him.

'You should have more confidence,' he said, 'in him and in yourself. If it feels right with him, then it probably is but he needs a little help, doesn't he?'

'What do you mean?' Janet asked.

'Has it occurred to you that he might be very much in love with you but reluctant to make a move because he thinks you're in love with someone else, because he sees that you're young and talented and ambitious?'

She gaped at him, trying to absorb these possibilities.

'If he is the scrupulous sort of man you have indicated that could well be the case.' He gave her his kindly, headmaster look. 'So that means that you have to offer a little assistance.'

'You mean not just to sit back and wait?' she asked.

'I did not think the young women of today just sat back and waited,' Harry said. 'I rather had the impression that they were bright independent spirits who were not afraid to 'do their own thing' — to coin a modern expression.'

Possibilities began to dawn in Janet's mind. Feelings of strength and self-assertion started to flow back.

'Is there any more advice,' she asked teasingly.

'Certainly not,' he said, 'I know better than to go further then sketching out the possibilities. Only you can do the fine brushwork.' He drummed a swift tune on the table and said briskly, 'Right then, let's get some tea made. I mustn't keep my wife waiting any longer!'

'Lucky wife!' Janet whispered to herself as Harry carried two steaming mugs away upstairs, his tread solid and dependable.

Janet had planned to travel back to the stables by train but her parents insisted on driving her. They set off early so Harry could be back in time for school.

It was not yet growing light as they unloaded cases from the car outside the cottage. Janet switched lights on and lit the logs in the fireplace to try to make the place seem cosier. It looked strange to her after two days' absence, sorry and desolate, as though it were burdened with all the loneliness and despair she had been feeling when she left it.

The December sky was just beginning to lighten as Phillippe's Porsche slid up the lane, sleek and black against the dawn, its engine growling softly as he nosed it against the courtyard wall. He came striding across towards the cottage.

'Hullo!' he said to Janet, 'you're back.'

'Yes.'

'Were you ill?' His tone was brusque, very much that of a boss to an employee.

'No — I needed a rest. I had quite a few days' leave due to me,' she said evenly, perfectly confident now about the best way to relate to him.

'Ah — yes. I badly need your help with the horses. We've got to ship them out to Germany — sooner than planned — and Brio seems to be off form, so I haven't had chance to get much work in on Princess at all.'

He looked rather desperate, as though he genuinely needed her support.

'Oh dear,' she said soothingly. 'I'll get Princess out right away.' She turned to her mother and Harry who were regarding the interchange with interest — Harry speculative, her mother simmering with excitement.

Janet made some courteously formal introductions. Immediately Phillippe lost his edginess. He saw that Janet's mother was one who liked to be charmed and he put himself out to be charming.

When he left them to make their private farewells, Janet's mother gazed after him.

'So handsome,' was all she whispered to Janet, but it was quite clear that she was thinking, he's lovely, he's eligible, he's wealthy, so couldn't you stop hankering after this Max person.

Janet grinned as she gave her mother a hug. 'Quite edible,' she agreed, 'but not the delicacy that suits me best.'

Vinnie would be proud of me she thought wryly. Her mother looked shocked, as though she felt that being unhappy in love required a more outwardly tragic commitment than her daughter was displaying.

'Mary!' Harry said sternly, 'we're going to be late!' As though on the end of an invisible thread, Mary climbed instantly into the passenger seat of the car, anxious not to cause her husband any annoyance.

Janet went back inside the cottage and began to gather her riding kit together. She picked up the one or two letters that lay on the mat and then noticed an envelope propped against a pile of books on the desk. Her name was written on it in bright violet ink. 'My sweet little friend,' it said inside, 'I have temporarily deserted you for warmer climates — gone off to search for the elusive Peter J.S. — couldn't bear another moment without him. Have a lovely, warm cuddly sort of Christmas and don't deny yourself any pleasures that may come your way — especially those of the gentlemanly variety with the long legs and the soft brown eyes. Madly jealous as always, darling, love and lots more love, see you before too long. V.'

It had obviously been written in a hurry. The writing roamed rather wildly across the page, punctuated by little smudges of nail varnish. Janet smiled to herself and opened the other mail. Amongst it was a plumpish packet with neat, unremarkable writing which she did not recognise. The postmark was London. Intrigued, Janet slit open the top. Inside was a bag of amaretti biscuits — not one in the slightest way crushed or broken. Her hands trembled as realisation began to dawn as to the identity of the sender. She searched for a letter. There was just a short note. 'I thought the prize-winning horse might appreciate a fresh supply of good things to eat. You might enjoy one or two as well. With my warm wishes, M.'

She read the words over and over

again, trying to find some hidden meaning, some sign of a very special personal affection but the message refused to convey more than a simple friendly regard.

She went to see Brio before going to tack up the Princess. He stood in his box, his great brown eyes hurt and wary-looking.

'Oh, poor boy,' she aid, 'what's the matter?' He pulled his silky muzzle away from her hand as she caressed him but his interest quickened as she rustled the paper in her pocket and brought out one of the bitter little biscuits.

'That's your delicacy, isn't it, lad?' she whispered, tickling the downy softness behind his ears. 'And what about me?' she thought, trying to recall the Baron's words on that first meeting, words about the importance of pleasure, of one's own special luxury. She felt unable to regard Max in that light; he was not a luxury, more a necessity, like water to drink or air to breathe.

'What am I going to do?' she asked

the disinterested Brio. 'How do I go about my fine brushwork?' She had already considered the possibilities, a telephone call or a letter perhaps. It was impossible to consider dropping in at the Thornlea. The house was right out in the country, not accessible at all without a car. A letter seemed rather formal, yet to telephone would require considerable courage.

'Talking to yourself?' an unmistakable voice drawled behind her. She turned and smiled, noting Phillippe's extreme physical handsomeness afresh and marvelling that it no longer excited her. He opened Brio's box and began to take the horse's rugs off in preparation for putting the saddle on.

'This horse smells of almonds!' he exclaimed. 'Are you still on with this personal delicacy nonsense?' he asked Janet crossly.

She apologised in a half-hearted fashion.

'My grandfather's still in bed,' he said. 'I'm running the show all on my own for once. It makes a change. Carry on with all this tit-bits business if you like, though, it makes no difference to me.' He shrugged his elegant shoulders and tacked up Brio with the swift efficiency of the expert.

'Bring the Princess up,' he said, 'and we'll work together on the routine for the competition.'

He was riding superbly that morning. Janet was once again lost in admiration. Whatever Brio had been miserable about seemed to have disappeared. He was working beautifully.

'You see,' Phillippe called as he circled around her, 'once he finds his balance he can conquer the world! But on some days I'm damned if he can do a thing.'

Janet put the Princess through a basic routine: a few loops, circles, some nice transitions of pace and then the more difficult exercises ending with the beautifully elevated, lengthened stride of the 'passage' gait.

Phillippe called to her, 'You're getting

to be a damn good rider. Your hands are just like elastic — beautiful!'

'Goodness, Phillippe — ' she called back, breathless with exertion, 'I've never had such praise from you!'

They worked solidly for an hour, alternatively watching each other and making critical comments. It seemed as though suddenly Phillippe had accepted her as a colleague — almost an equal.

She tackled him directly as they walked with the horses back to their boxes. 'Am I riding in the competition in Holland or not?' she said.

'Why not?' he said. 'There's always got to be a first time. I've booked a ticket for you anyway.'

'Weren't you going to tell me?' she asked curiously — 'if I hadn't asked myself, I mean.'

'Oh, yes.' His tone was casual.

'You weren't!' she complained. 'You're a dark horse.'

He laughed. It was odd, she reflected, how they could be so friendly. Phillippe appeared quite recovered from his feelings of rejection and now that she no longer spent all her time wondering how best to humour him, they seemed to get along very well.

Her spirits considerably renewed by the morning's work she decided to telephone Max after lunch. She had no definite plan of what she would say, the important thing was to let him know that she did not consider their relationship at an end, that she was thinking of him, that he was important to her.

A rather prim female voice answered.

'Oh,' she faltered, 'could I speak to Mr Thornton, please?'

'Mr Thornton's away at present.'

'Oh.'

'Do you want to make a booking?' the voice said.

'Er — no.' This was more difficult than she had anticipated.

'Is there any message I can take for you?'

'No, not really. Could you tell me when he will be back?'

'The day after tomorrow — about six o?clock.'

'Oh, I see.'

'Will that be all?'

Indecision. 'Will you please tell him that Janet Holt telephoned.'

'Certainly — do you wish him to call you back?'

Oh goodness! 'Er — no — I may be on my way to Holland when he gets back. I'll call another time.'

'I see. Well, Miss Holt, I will make sure he gets your message. Good-bye.'

Janet stared into the phone as it clicked and then droned out its dialling tone. 'And good-bye to you,' she thought, wondering where Max had found such a fiercely efficient-sounding lady.

Her disappointment was considerable but not crippling. At least I've made a start at doing something, she thought.

She drove her energies into her riding for the next two days. She and Phillippe worked almost without let up, devising a full exhibition routine for Brio and the Princess. Each horse had four schooling sessions a day — gruelling for animal and rider alike. In addition there was extra work to be done in caring for the other horses in the stables as many of the riding school students who carried out the routine tasks were at home for the Christmas period. Yet she and Phillippe seemed able to work tirelessly with the minimum of rest.

On the afternoon before they were due to set off for Holland, Phillippe invited Janet to watch his finally worked-out routine with Brio. It turned out to be one of those grim days when nothing seemed to go right. Phillippe's mood seemed dark and gradually turned to black anger when the horse refused to respond adequately to his aids. Janet was puzzled by this swift and marked change in Phillippe's whole demeanour. He had appeared so at ease with the world during the past two days. She supposed that unrelenting effort and the terrible frustration of Brio's lack of co-operation must account for it.

But her puzzlement turned to alarm as she noted a flicker of savagery in his face as he cantered down the length of the school towards her. She was sitting in the spectators' gallery so that she had an advantageous view of the detailed movements of both horse and rider. She saw the hovering uncertainty of Brio's gait, the restriction in his stride; the shiver of terror as he felt the razor sharpness of Phillippe's spurs on his velvety flanks. It was usual practice to ride with spurs for precision competition work but the actual use was minimal. Janet had never found any need for them with the Princess and she suspected that she would not need them with Brio either.

Brio's performance grew no better and the punishment grew more bitter. Janet saw glistening red threads appear on Brio's sides, bright marks of violence on that shiny copper-beech coat. She closed her eyes in grief. 'Oh, Phillippe,' she whispered, 'you'll destroy him; he will never do anything for you now.'

She called out in firm tones, 'Stop it, Phillippe, he's bleeding.'

He turned in fury. 'Get out!' he yelled, his voice crazy with anger. 'Leave me alone. I'll fight my own battles.'

She sat, rooted to the spot in horror.

'Go on,' he shouted, 'get out, clear off, get lost — just let me do things my way for once.' She stood up in despair and did as he asked.

She went back to the cottage and forced herself to eat something. It was 5.30. They were due to set off the next day to travel to the ferry. The horses would not enjoy the travelling particularly but Brio would not be fit for anything if he set off in an upset state. It was absolutely vital that a horse finished his exercises on a happy and successful note. Putting an unhappy horse back in his box meant bringing him out unhappy next time.

At seven o'clock she was unable to

resist the longing to go and find out if Brio was comfortable. She approached his box, talking gently, and rustling paper in her pocket to let him know she had some of his favourite biscuits.

He shifted uneasily.

'It's all right, lad,' she crooned to him.

He allowed her to feed him the biscuits, but the slightest unexpected movement of Janet's filled him with undisguised fear. He laid his ears back and she saw the white glint of his eyes. She flicked the switch on the outside of the box and a weak bulb in the ceiling of the stall threw down a pale yellow light, enabling her to examine Brio's quarters. But there was nothing to see; he was well covered with rugs against the sharp December night.

As she slipped quietly inside the box the horse's reaction of fear almost unnerved her. He shifted with such a rush of anxiety that she thought he might crush her. 'There, there,' she said, trying to give him the confidence

268

which had almost deserted her. She lifted the rugs and looked at his flanks. The cuts had been well-washed and almost merged with the dark brown hair. But Janet, who had felt every sting as though she had received them herself, could identify each abrasion. 'It's all right, I won't touch,' she murmured, replacing the rugs. She fondled the horse a little, feeling that it was important to try to re-establish his trust in human beings. She judged that it was his confidence that had been wounded, the physical damage was negligible.

She returned to the cottage and completed her packing. She wished she could feel excited but a heavy sensation of foreboding had the upper hand.

Phillippe telephoned her at eight o'clock. 'I'm going out,' he said, his voice calm and subdued, as though the outburst of a few hours ago was of no importance. 'Can you hold the fort? The Baron's still groggy and anyone else with any sense seems to be on holiday.' She smiled at the jagged-edged compliment.

'I'll be fine — don't worry,' she said reassuringly. 'Have a good time,' she added.

'Yes,' doubtfully, 'I will.' He rang off.

His car swooped round the curve in the courtyard a few minutes later. Janet wondered where he was going, with whom, whether he was meeting someone on business or going to a party perhaps.

She picked up the phone again, her finger hovering on the dial. Max might not be back yet and in any case a conversation with him might upset the delicate emotional balance she had managed to achieve over the last few days. Better to wait until she returned from Holland. It was only another four days — and she might have some interesting news to tell him.

As is often the case, going to bed early did not result in getting extra sleep. At eleven o'clock Janet switched on the light and swung her legs out of bed. She could not get Brio out of her mind, could not help feeling that his chances of any success in a big competition were ruined unless his confidence was restored.

Pushing back the full implications of her proposed actions she dressed quickly and set off towards the tack room.

Brio seemed calmer than previously and gave Janet a few exploratory nuzzles as she slipped his saddle on as gently as she could.

'Greedy,' she said, 'you can have a biscuit later.'

They walked steadily together to the schooling arena, hooves and feet making a soft flup flup sound on the sodden ground. Brio stood patiently whilst Janet searched in the blackness for the floodlight switches. Once in the arena his nervousness reasserted itself, he laid his ears back, danced a little when she wanted him to stand, moved away as she tightened the girth. She took his head in her arms. 'I'm not

271

going to hurt,' she told him. 'We're just going to do some very gentle exercises because you're a wonderful horse and you've got to remember that all the way in the horse box and on the ferry and in the competition ring. O.K.?' she queried, breathing softly into his nostrils. He stood perfectly calmly now, his eyes peaceful, his ears cocked and alert. Trying to shed thoughts of anything but the horse's welfare she took up the reins, put her foot in the stirrup and lightly swung herself on to his back.

He turned out to be everything she had ever dreamed a horse could be and more. Whereas the Princess responded to the mere thought of a command Brio actively engendered new ideas in his rider by means of his range and accuracy of movement. He had an instinctive feel for balance and symmetry; his extended movements had a loftiness about them which thrilled Janet with pure delight. Once he was warmed up and his confidence regained, all she had to do was maintain a correct position and follow the rhythmic beauty of his movements. She could feel each fluid harmonic ripple of his neck and quarters echo through her own body.

The intensity of her exhilaration robbed her of all sense of time. Midnight came and went and still they were working; horse and rider inextricably blended in a unity of purpose and pleasure. She began to feel that together they were invincible, they could conquer the world. She could not finish without attempting the difficult piaffer movement, that wonderful elevated suspension of the horse's mass between the beats of his hoofs as he trotted on the spot, the exercise which Brio and Phillippe seemed to find elusive. She prepared carefully, anxious to help him have his head, neck and quarters aligned so as to be in perfect balance. At the mid-point of the arena as they trotted diagonally from one side to the other she gently asked the horse for this last and splendid effort. He responded with courtesy and precision and as she glanced across to the large mirror hanging on the planked wall she saw a perfect example of the exercise, the stride magnificently and markedly lofty, the suspension breathtakingly tense, the striking of the ground with the hoofs wholly accurate.

She moved him away to the edge of the arena, urging him into an active trot to finish the session. Suddenly the sound of clapping struck out into the chill air. It seemed to come from the blackness of the spectators' gallery. A piercing, spinning coil of fear shot through her chest.

There was only a temporary slackening of fear as she watched Phillippe step out of the shadows into the flood-lights, for now there was a sudden terror as to the safety of her whole career as she looked at his face and read its expression.

He was in evening dress, smoking a cigar and swaggering extravagantly. The glitter in his eyes suggested that he had been drinking quite heavily. She was to discover that alcohol accentuated the less attractive aspects of his personality.

'So,' he drawled. 'Little Miss Pure and Perfect has her faults after all just like the rest of us.'

Impossible to reply, she felt. She slipped off Brio's back and prepared to run the stirrup irons up.

Phillippe watched. He had evidently been enjoying himself and seemed to have every intention of going on doing so.

'I thought I'd take a look at Brio when I got back,' he said, eyeing her sardonically, a faintly playful smile on his lips. 'But he seemed to have disappeared. I must admit I was a little worried.' He put the cigar to his lips, drew on it, blew the smoke into a lazy curl, mused a little. 'I could see the headlines: 'Priceless top-class horse snatched from stables hours before international dressage event'. It could have sent my grandfather to an early grave.'

His expression had changed to one of gentle, mischievous chiding.

'However,' he continued, 'it occurred to me that you, my sweet, might have had similar thoughts about taking a look at our mutual top-class friend. So . . . ' he paused tantalisingly, 'I came straight along here. You were so absorbed; you never suspected you had company, did you?'

There was no point in her making any protest.

'I must say, Janet, you certainly have turned into a pretty passable rider. There are still one or two points that need sorting out . . . but,' another pause.

She pressed her lips together, hunched her shoulders slightly in an automatic gesture of self-protection. What was he going to do? There was some obvious intent in his mind already. He was just indulging in a little game of cat and mouse to amuse himself and prolong the suspension.

Suddenly he vaulted across the

balcony which separated the spectators from the arena. He stood close to her, his virile maleness overwhelming her; the strong finely tuned body, the delicately powerful hands, the piercing gaze in the handsome tanned face. For a swift moment she wondered if he was going to promise silence and forgiveness in return for sexual surrender. Oh God!

'Well now,' he said cheerfully, 'it's not going to look too good when I tell the Baron, is it. And I will have to tell him. After all, anything could have happened; could still happen.' He turned to the horse. 'He could go lame, couldn't he?' he commented, running an expert hand over Brio's hocks, 'or have a chill? He's not used to working at one o'clock in the morning. It could all be very distressing just before the competition. Embarrassing as well for our dealings with the insurance company who would want full details. The good name of the stables would be at stake.'

He did not need to go on. She was

fully aware of the ramifications of her impulsive action. Phillippe's words sounded laden with doom. She would have to leave the stables — there would be no future for her here. It was as simple as that.

'And then,' he said thoughtfully, 'there's the question of references for another position.' It was clear that as far as he was concerned she would not be getting any bouquets. A cold wave of despair overtook her. Not only to leave — but to leave in desperate disgrace. Her riding career would reach an abrupt end. No one would trust her any more.

'Don't say anything else, Phillippe,' she said, her voice full of dull lethargy. 'I'll put Brio away now. That's the least I can do.'

She made her way to the door with as much dignity as she could dredge up. Phillippe helpfully closed up the arena and switched off the lights before disappearing into the darkness.

'Goodbye, darling,' Janet said thickly

to Brio when she had rugged him up for what remained of the night. 'Whatever else happens — you've given me a memory I shall treasure for always.' It might have felt good to shed warm tears on his neck, but nothing would come. Inside she was as cold and dead as marble.

Alone again in the cottage her mind was cleared of everything except escape and flight. She could not stay a moment longer. She began to pack her cases, heaving them from the top of a wardrobe with the perverse strength that comes from hopelessness.

By five o'clock she had everything ready in the tiny hallway. She realised the impossibility of trying to cope with it all herself and humped it back upstairs. Her mother would come over later to collect it. She found she could not plan anything at the moment — explanatory messages to the Baron, a note for Vinnie, a formal apology to Phillippe. She must just go — and no one must see her.

She dressed warmly for the two-mile walk to the bus. The morning was bitterly cold with a dull, grey, heavy frost. Carrying just her shoulder bag and a small hold-all, she made her way along the deserted country road. The chill began to eat into her and she quickened her pace to try to stimulate warmth. As the road dipped down towards the river a thick fog enveloped her. She went steadily on, a little anxious at being so vulnerable walking along a narrow road with no pavement.

The soft droning of a car's engine sounded in the distance. Her heartbeats quickened. She tucked herself well into the side of the road, scratching her cheek on the briars sticking through the hedge. The car seemed to be proceeding cautiously — obviously not Phillippe pursuing her in his Porsche she thought with grim humour. It drew level, slowed right down, passed her and then stopped, its brilliant fog lamps striking out into the freezing mist.

Despite the mental fog of wretched-ness and fatigue she instantly recognised the curved lines of the shiny blue boot and watched with overpower-ing relief as a tall man with wavy brown hair and unforgettably kind eyes got out and walked towards her.

Instantly the tears were there, spring-ing from somewhere in her chest, pushing into her throat and veiling her eyes. She did not give him chance to speak before hurling herself at him with all the violence of grief and frustration she had kept locked in herself during the last few dreadful hours.

'Oh, Max!' she said before breaking into a storm of weeping which tossed and shook her body as a night wind drives the trees in whirling darkness.

He held her tight, murmuring her name softly, pinning her to him with one arm; ruffling her hair with his free hand, rubbing her shoulders, stroking her back.

She was dimly aware of his speaking to her — something about always being around to share her worst moments. She did not care what he said, it was enough just to have him there.

'We can't stay here,' he said, pushing her gently towards the car.

He appeared quite relaxed behind the wheel despite the sudden appearance of a distraught young woman and a range of visibility extending to no more than a few yards.

She tried to tell him things but only gasping, shuddering, sobs emerged.

'Let me do the talking,' he said, smiling at her. 'I've been in London buying wines, spent the day at Heathrow waiting for the fog to clear and eventually came back on the night train, had to take a taxi to collect my car at the airport and here I am, unshaven and breakfastless, driving home about fourteen hours later than I should be.'

She gazed at him, mournful and adoring, forgetting that her eyes were a mess of plumped-up, slithering redness.

He said softly, 'I've never been so glad I got held up before. What on earth would you have done trudging all this way up the road in freezing fog if I hadn't come along?' He grinned at her. He seemed in no hurry to ask questions, he simply accepted her presence and seemed glad of it.

'If you're not in a hurry to go anywhere perhaps you would like to join me for breakfast,' he said solemnly, glancing briefly at her.

She felt the genuine spark of a smile break through her misery. 'I'd love to join you for breakfast,' she said, the smile growing a little — lunch and dinner too, she thought, and bed and breakfast would be even better. A definite flicker of interest in the future seemed to be growing again inside her.

'What's the joke?' he asked patiently. 'You're leaving me out again.'

'Nothing,' she murmured, sinking back into the velvety seats and enjoying the rush of air pouring from the heating vents.

She refused to think seriously about

anything until they reached the Thorn-lea, giving herself up fully to the comfort of the quietly purring car and the wonderful security of Max's presence. Now that she was with him she had an overwhelming sensation that he loved her, wanted her as much as she wanted him. It was as though she had built up great hurdles between them, whereas in reality there were no more than little steps to be taken in order to bring them together.

It took Max exactly twenty minutes to produce a breakfast of eggs, bacon, toast and coffee. They ate it in the kitchen of his flat — a long, slim pine-clad room full of cookery books and plants. He talked to her about his visit to London; about his plans to open a wine bar in the town; about the restaurant. Not until she had finished her meal did he allow thought or conversation about anything else.

'Now,' he said, 'do you want to tell?'

She told, giving a graphic account of the previous night's happenings.

'It was a dreadful thing to do, Max. To ride someone else's first-rate horse without their permission is bad enough but to take the risks I took just before a big event. Well . . . it's unforgivable. No one will trust me now.'

'I see.' He nodded. 'And you say the horse went very well for you?'

'Yes — ' She was surprised at this line of questioning.

'You could ride him in Holland, do well there I mean?'

'Yes, I suppose so!'

'Better than Phillippe?'

'No' — doubtfully.

'But probably as well as Phillippe and perhaps better than Phillippe on a bad day.'

She stared. 'Yes.'

He pondered. 'So you achieved what you had planned, didn't you?'

'What do you mean?'

'You restored the horse's confidence and proved his capabilities of doing well in a top-level competition. In other words you did nothing but good.'

She had not quite regarded it in that light. 'Yes . . . but think of the risk!'

'Risk?' he chuckled, running a hand over his unshaven chin, 'if no one took risks we'd all die of stagnation!'

She was still not convinced.

'Courage!' he said. 'What you must do is go back straight away, do some hard explaining, then go and win some rosettes in Holland.'

She gazed at him horror-stricken.

'I can't!'

'Yes, you can.' He stood up decisive, purposeful, energetic. 'I'm going to shave, and then I'm going to drive you there,' he said. 'I'll give you fifteen minutes to get yourself in the right frame of mind — oh, and there's a shower room in the guest room if you're feeling really brave on a cold morning like this.'

He went off humming. He was simply refusing to share her extreme despondency. She supposed he had always taken that approach to difficult situations — looking for the active and positive way to improve things.

Max's shower room was temptingly warm despite the freezing temperatures outside. She slipped her clothes off and stood under the hot jets of water, luxuriating in the scented steaminess inside the cubicle. The soft droplets caressed her into temporary relaxation. It was painfully tantalising to be standing there naked with Max so close by and yet still so separate from her. Although enormously grateful for his encouragement and support she felt a growing despair that he had not crushed her in his arms, re-awakened her purpose to fight back by taking her to bed and making her feel wonderful and wanted. She wrapped herself in one of his huge, fluffy towels and considered going to him now — just as she was. She knew he would not reject her.

Then she looked in the mirror, saw her face pale and puffy, the nose shiny and pinkish, eyes streaked with the grey remnants of smudged, mascara-stained tears.

I look about as sexy as a pregnant sheep, she thought, recalling one of Vinnie's phrases. She rubbed herself dry and dressed again. Courage seemed to drain away as each garment went on. She could not go back — she just could not face it. She wanted to stay here, unchallenged and safe.

She rushed out of the room and knocked urgently on Max's door. He came straight away. He was wearing a short kimono-style robe, droplets of water glistened on his skin and his hair was damp. He had obviously stepped straight out of the bath.

'I'm sorry,' she muttered.

'Are you all right?' he asked, quite unperturbed, pulling her into the room and sitting her down on the bed.

'I can't go,' she said.

He looked stern. 'Nonsense.'

'No — really I can't. Let me stay here, Max,' she burst out impulsively. 'I'll be a waitress, wash up, do anything!' She was shocked at the pleading tone in her voice.

'Certainly not.' His tone was cold. He was angry now.

She did not know which offer he was refusing. Did it matter? It was all so hopeless — she had ruined everything.

'I'm going to get dressed,' he said, 'and then I'm taking you to the stables and leaving you there. I've a lot of work to do here and I must get back quickly.' He was watching her carefully; he was always watching, never avoiding sensitive issues, always ready to meet her eyes. He smiled gently and his voice softened. 'You can ring me,' he said, 'when you've got yourself fully sorted out and your case packed for Holland.'

He came and knelt down by her. It was a sudden and totally unexpected gesture which sent her mind reeling. 'Look,' he said, 'you women, I don't understand you. You want to be so independent and at the first breath of trouble you're going to pieces and running for shelter under some man's umbrella. Well, I never use umbrellas

— I think it does good to get a little wet sometimes.'

'Oh, Max!'

'You're going,' he said, 'and that's that!'

He got up and went across to the wardrobe, preparing to shed his robe as he went. He had not asked her to leave but she fled, her heart beating violently with desire at the thought of his magnificent, powerful body. She had not failed to notice the long curved muscles of his arms and thighs, the strong bone structure just visible through the covering of flesh on his chest as he sat talking to her.

She waited for him in the more neutral atmosphere of the kitchen, her mind a cocophony of images and impressions, misery, elation, fear, shame and a desperate physical hunger which clawed at her insides; a throbbing, insistent, relentless pain.

In the car she was unable to speak; the fear kept rising in her throat.

As they reached the stables he said,

'Now you know what to do. You must put the record straight with both the Baron and Phillippe; you must make sure you're going to Holland as planned and that your contract runs unchanged until the end of January as previously agreed.' It was the lawyer in him speaking, cool, detached and thorough.

'Yes,' her voice sounded faint and far away. He pulled the car up, then leaned across and opened the door. She made a grab as his face came close to hers and pressed a fierce kiss on him. It landed somewhere around his left ear. He smiled.

'Good luck!' he said giving her a playful wink and an encouraging squeeze of the hand. She stood watching as the car moved down the lane, its white exhaust fumes curling mysteriously into the fog. Soon there were just two pin-points of light in the distance.

The warning note of the engine lingered in her ears long after the sound had died from the air.

She went straight to the Baron's house and knocked on the door of his office although she did not really expect to find him there as he was reputedly not fully recovered from his illness. She looked at her watch. It was two minutes before eleven. The rattle of wheels and cups could be heard approaching from one of the rooms behind the hallway. The Baron's housekeeper appeared, pushing a trolley on which stood a coffee pot, and an assortment of mouth-watering cakes.

'He is in there,' she said to Janet, in that careful, deliberate way of speaking English that is characteristic of those who have a different native language. 'He will not hear you knock. He sleeps a lot just at the moment.'

'Is he better?' Janet asked anxiously.

'Oh, very much better. He will be happy to see you. He often speaks to me about you,' she smiled.

'Oh.' Janet felt a glow of warm surprise.

The Baron was sitting beside the fire,

muffled in sweaters and a scarf. His head jerked up as he heard the rumble of the trolley. 'Ah,' he said, a smile spreading as his eyes travelled over the cakes. He looked up and saw Janet. The smile grew. 'My dear, how good of you to come. Sit down, sit down.' He gestured eagerly to the chair opposite his. His housekeeper looked at him anxiously. 'You are feeling well today?'

'Yes, much better — please,' he asked, patting her hand, 'another cup and saucer for the young lady?'

'I was just going to fetch it!' she said reassuringly.

'You really are feeling better,' Janet said, leaning forward towards the Baron, realising that he thought her call was a social one, reading the delight in his eyes and wishing that she had come to see him sooner.

'Oh, yes. I have only had a virus but I must take care of my heart. The doctor is very stern but he does not forbid chocolate cake,' he said with the wicked smile of a small boy. 'Now, my dear,' he continued, eyeing her thoughtfully, 'you should be preparing for Holland. You leave in about half an hour I believe.'

It was quite obvious that he knew nothing of last night's events. Was this a good or a bad sign? Best to come straight to the point, whatever the case.

'Baron, last night I,' she hesitated, unsure that this was the best beginning, 'last night . . . '

He was concentrating hard, staring into her face. 'My dear, you need not be afraid of me — not ever.'

'I took Brio up to the arena at eleven o'clock at night and rode him for almost two hours.' Stated simply, like that, it did not sound such a terrible thing.

'Ah.' A fresh gleam of boyish wickedness appeared in his eyes. 'And how did he do for you?' She stared at him, recalling that Max had used almost identical words.

'He went well,' she said, 'very well in fact.'

He nodded. 'Yes, he would,' he

agreed, eyes twinkling.

The second cup and saucer arrived to interrupt the dialogue. With coffee poured and a slice of Black Forest cake in front of each of them they resumed the conversation.

'Is it very bad?' she asked him. 'Should I leave?'

It was his turn to stare. 'My dear!' he protested, 'you have been a little naughty but I'm sure there was a reason and there is no one in the world I would trust my Brio with more than you.' He paused, looking at her with grandfatherly sternness. 'But you must never repeat that outside this room.'

She could visualise Phillippe's stricken, angry face, should he ever hear those words. 'No,' she agreed, 'no!'

'I want to think,' he said. 'It will do me good to get my brains working again. Just eat, my dear — enjoy yourself. You are far too thin.'

She did as he told her, savouring the splendid Kirsch-soaked cake and the hot, sharp freshness of the coffee.

'I think,' he said after a few minutes, 'that Phillippe must be involved in this. He has been having a very difficult time recently. He has been unloved and unhappy. It will have affected his riding, I know; I remember him as a child. He will have become frustrated and matters will have gone from bad to worse — yes?'

'Yes.'

He nodded. 'Yes, I can see it all. You will have had a very bad night, my dear. Very bad. And all you wanted to do was make a wretched horse happy again!'

He fell silent and she sat with him, quite relaxed now, reassured by his calm perception and judgment.

Suddenly he said, 'Someone must have suggested you should leave. I can guess everything — but I would prefer it to remain unspoken even between the two of us. My dear — will you trust me when I say that things will be better from now on. You have my full trust and confidence still. Your very distress shows me what a trustworthy person you are.' He stopped, a smile on his lips. 'There is a lot of talk of trust, is there not? I think that is all that matters. Now you go and pack your things. You have a very important competition to go to.'

She listened, was grateful, almost fully reassured. 'My contract?' she said apologetically, questioning him with her eyes.

'Your contract, my dear,' he said, 'remains where it always has, secure and unaltered in my safe.' He sighed. 'I'm a little tired now,' he said. 'I shall have to send you away.'

She rose to shake the hand he held out. Instead he took her hand to his lips and kissed it. His lips were soft and dry, printing no mark on her skin. She knelt by him and took his hand to her cheek, pressing it there and smiling into his eyes. She could tell that he was pleased, that she had brought a glow to his day.

And so the interview that she had dreaded had turned out like a dream rather than a nightmare. Not only had she been forgiven but she had learned how valued she was in the Baron's eyes, how much her work and effort had pleased him. It was hard not to leap and shout with joy in the hallway. She managed a decorous exit from the quietness of the house and then leapt and skipped across the cobbles towards the cottage until she felt the thin, treacherous layer of ice underfoot and slowed herself down. This was no time for a broken leg.

She burst into the cottage and noticed that lights were on in the sitting room. With amazement she saw Vinnie and Phillippe sitting together on the sofa. They had that bolt upright, just-sprung-apart look of people who have been kissing each other at length and in depth.

Phillippe said, 'Janet! Thank God.' And then, 'Where the hell have you been?'

'Trying to sort myself out,' she said drily.

He ran a hand through his hair

distractedly. Vinnie looked on with lazy amusement. She was in a mood for sitting back and enjoying the action. Janet decided not to disappoint her.

'You convinced me,' she told Phillippe. 'I really thought I'd burned my boats. I was all packed up to leave. I set off in fact.'

'Oh God,' he groaned. 'I was tight. I was over the top, behaving like a fool.'

'Actually you were rather splendid at playing the villain,' Janet said calmly, feeling that she had grown up years in the last twenty-four hours. 'I met Max Thornton. He rescued me like people do in books. He made me see things from a rather different angle.'

Phillippe and Vinnie were listening intently now.

'And I've been to see the Baron,' she said. 'Don't be alarmed, Phillippe, I didn't spell out what happened last night, but he guesses most of it. As you once said, Vinnie, he's no fool.'

She paused to allow them time to give her words full consideration. 'The important thing is that he understands why things happened as they did and he forgives us both.'

'Well, darling — you're certainly not pulling any punches this morning,' Vinnie said. 'It's obvious that this new fiancé of mine is rather a dark horse — he never told me a thing!'

Janet was not surprised at the news. Even whilst talking of her own problems her mind had been racing along other pathways, arriving at the conclusion that Vinnie and Phillippe had at last faced up to loving each other. It was as though she had known it all along but had never let herself realise it consciously.

'Congratulations!' she said, smiling warmly at both of them.

'He's hardly the new improved version,' Vinnie said. 'Peter J. S. was really a much better bet. It's just that this one,' giving Phillippe a slap on his elegant hips, 'has been under my skin for too long. I need him about as much as a jockey needs a broken arm but I can't do without him.'

Phillippe returned the slap. 'I'm the only one who can possibly handle her,' he said without a trace of sentimentality.

'Phillippe,' Janet said abruptly, 'I'm going to Holland.'

'Yes,' he nodded, 'of course.'

'And I'm riding Princess.'

'Yes.'

'That's all right then.'

Phillippe offered her his hand. 'I'm sorry,' he said simply, and she knew that many incidents from the last few months were included in that apology. Things were working out so well, she could hardy believe it. But there was still a terrible ache of emptiness to mar the wellbeing. At least she could telephone him now and tell him of her achievements.

Phillippe was looking at his watch. He said, 'I have to go now — literally this minute.'

'Oh, help — I'm not ready!' Janet exclaimed.

Vinnie and Phillippe exchanged glances.

'Janet can't go with you,' Vinnie said. 'She needs at least an hour to pack. I'll ring and book her a flight out to Amsterdam.'

Janet laughed in surprise.

'Too foggy,' Phillippe said agitatedly. 'There'll be no flights today.'

'I'll have to come on a later ferry,' Janet said, feeling more calm and resourceful than both her companions put together. 'I'll ring and book now.'

She soon had everything fixed up. Phillippe had left by the time she came off the phone. She could hear the horse trailer trundling down the lane.

She dialled the Thornlea. Warmth spread through her limbs at the obvious pleasure in Max's voice as they talked.

'I don't really like to say 'I told you so',' he said.

'I'm so glad you were there to give me the courage,' said. 'It could have been a disaster if I hadn't made an effort and I don't think I would have

302

done it on my own.'

'Fate,' he said dismissively. 'When are you going to Holland?'

She outlined the travel details.

'I'll drive you to the ferry,' he said. Her heart leapt.

'I thought you were busy.'

'I am, but some things are more important even than work,' he commented. 'I'll pick you up in an hour — O.K.?'

'O.K.' she confirmed.

'Aha,' said Vinnie, who had been openly eaves-dropping, 'so things are full steam ahead with the lovely Max, are they?'

'Mmm,' Janet mused, 'no comment! So you're not in love with him any more I take it?' she asked mischievously.

'Oh, still a teeny bit, pet. Who wouldn't be?'

'And has it been Phillippe all the time?' Janet asked, eyeing her friend with admiration. The kisses had left her glowing from her tousled auburn curls down to her bare crimson-toed feet.

'Oh, yes — afraid so. We were in love in the cradle practically. I broke it all off just before you came, though. He got desperately moody about the riding, especially when his sister was doing so well on the international dressage circuit. He was always either working or sulking. I met Peter J. S. on a holiday in Greece in the spring and he simply couldn't resist me and I simply couldn't resist him and his money and his worshipful attention. You know I need lots of applause, darling. Well, he was like a permanently ecstatic first-night audience. Then, of course, when I came back to Yorkshire I never saw him but I *did* see the in-laws-to-be unfortunately. That weekend I went to stay was the limit. I came back early on the Sunday and Phillippe and I made it up a little. And incidentally that's how I knew about the competition before you did. Phil was full of it. After that I was a bit naughty and turned cool again, decided to have a final meeting with Peter J. S.

So poor Phillippe was really dangling for a while.'

And tried to heal his wounds with me, Janet thought, feeling immensely sympathetic towards Phillippe.

'I tried to persuade myself I wasn't still in love, encouraging you with Phillippe, but I had to keep opening up the safety valve by teasing you about Max. And I did feel I'd made a tremendous effort by getting engaged to Peter J. S. in the first place. And none of it worked! This last weekend I went to Paris to sort things out finally with Peter. It was jolly tough going. I promised Phillippe I would telegraph him with a definite 'engagement to Peter on or off message' before eight o'clock yesterday evening, but all the lines were jammed and I couldn't get through.'

'He was rather upset,' Janet said wryly, recalling the Phillippe of the night before.

'Yes — poor lamb, but I did move heaven and earth to get back to him. I came on about the only flight operating in the whole of Europe yesterday — just got into the North East Airport before the fog arrived. Phillippe came up to meet me in the middle of the night — the poppet was still in evening dress. I just kept on kissing him, it seemed the best thing to do.' She yawned delicately. 'And now I'm totally shattered. I'm going to sleep and sleep in my lovely cosy bed.'

'Good,' said Janet, 'that's you sorted out. Now I've got to pack.'

Vinnie sat and watched the packing. She was curious. 'Just what did happen last night, pet?' she asked. 'Phillippe was pretty up-tight about your disappearance.'

'It was one of those times,' Janet said carefully, 'when people's emotions overrule their judgment — sorry to sound pompous!'

'Wow — I'm impressed,' Vinnie said — 'in other words, you're not telling!'

'That's right.'

Vinnie sat for a while. 'You're a

treasure, little will o' the wisp, Janet,' she said, 'a real rock-solid diamond.'

'Thanks!'

'You know you've caused Phil to do quite a bit of soul-searching one way and another, sweetie,' Vinnie said casually. 'I think at one point he was wondering if you were going to take over the number one riding spot. The Baron was very impressed with little Janet and her peaceful hands.'

'Oh God!' Janet groaned, 'it must have been hell for him.'

'But he gave you a bit back, didn't he, darling? Remember that day on Chiefie at the spooky old house?'

Janet suddenly realised what tormented jealousy had lain behind Phillippe's actions.

'I gave him hell after that little lot!' Vinnie said fervently. 'You're too precious to be messed around like that.' She paused, considered, smiled mischievously and went on: 'I hope Max realises what a gem you are — but I'm sure he does — I'm convinced *his* judgement is well equipped to combat his emotions — but let's hope not too much so. A little loss of manly reasoning and control is necessary sometimes.'

Flippant words, casually tossed away yet with a deep ring of truth, Janet thought as she closed the lid of her case.

She was not quite ready when Max arrived so that he had the full benefit of an exuberant hug from Vinnie, swiftly followed up by an announcement of her intention to marry Phillippe before the New Year was very old.

'Well — congratulations!' Janet heard him say as she ran down the stairs, bumping case and bags against the wall in her hurry.

'Ah — the new young hope of the international dressage scene,' Vinnie drawled.

'Oh, help!' Janet said.

Max was standing very still, a quiet, calm, steadying figure in the midst of all the feverish excitement of the last few hours.

'Something of a responsibility being a new young hope,' he said lightly, his eyes alight with tender concern as he noted Janet's pale face with its air of suppressed tension and anticipation.

He put her and her things in the car, gave Vinnie a sudden, roguish hug which even she had some difficulty withstanding and then they were off.

A mile or two went by in comparative silence.

'Are you all right?' he asked softly after a time.

She smiled into his eyes. 'Yes,' she whispered.

'You could go to sleep if you liked.'

'No!' There were two hours before the boat went. She wanted to live them to the full.

He asked her to tell him again about her interview with the Baron, interested to pursue each detail, examine the full meaning behind all that was said.

'It seems to me,' he said slowly, 'that the Baron has a very high opinion of you, both as a person and as a rider.'

'Yes, I think he does,' she said.

'Is there any future in it?' he asked.

'There could be,' she said slowly, 'but I'm not sure that I want it any more.'

'Of course you do,' he said sharply.

'No,' she said calmly, 'I'm not at all convinced that I want to spend my time in competition work on other people's horses.'

'You need a sponsor,' he said.

'Perhaps.'

He fell silent again; he seemed to have dived deep into his own thoughts.

'So Phillippe and Vinnie have got together at last?' he said.

'Yes,' she chuckled.

'I'd always wondered about that.'

'What do you mean?'

'Those two — I thought they were trying a little too hard to ignore each other.'

'Oh . . . *I* never really guessed. I must have been blinkered.'

'You had other things on your mind?'

She thought about it. 'Plenty really!'

'So . . . Vinnie and Phillippe go off together into the sunset?' he said.

She laughed. 'I suppose so.'

He turned to her. 'And does that hurt?' he asked, his eyes filled with tenderness, so that she was instantly disarmed, unable to hold back any longer. What was the point anyway. She loved him so much — what was there to lose by letting him know. 'Max,' she said gently, 'there is only one man who could hurt me by being attached to someone else and you must know by now who he is.'

He paused, his eyes on the road ahead, tracing its central white line through the mist.

'I didn't dare to believe it,' he said evenly. 'I've been hurt badly before.'

A glow of warmth spread through her as the full meaning of his words became unmistakably clear.

'I won't hurt you,' she said. 'At least I'll try very hard not to.' She reached out and touched his cheek softly with her fingertips. He grasped her and kissed each finger lightly, running the warmth of his lips along her hand.

'We'll stop for a minute,' he said. 'My concentration seems to have gone!'

They were on the edge of moorland where there were just miles of tufted grey misted grass merging into the laden, dripping sky. The car could be tucked away from the road on the mossy strips which formed a threshold between grass and tarmac.

With the purr of the engine switched off, the silence and emptiness were almost overpowering.

'Just you and me,' she whispered, 'all alone in the world.'

He leaned towards her and she put her hands around his face and pulled it down to hers. He kissed her as though he did not mean ever to let her out of his sight again.

'I've wasted an awful lot of time,' he murmured, nibbling her ear.

'You certainly have!' she chided, slipping her hand inside his jacket and feeling the solid massive warmth of his chest, before renewing her efforts at kissing him.

After a time he pulled away a little and grinned.

'That's not kissing,' he said, 'that's devouring. What a hungry girl you are.'

She nodded. 'But you like it, don't you?' she asked.

'Oh, yes!' he said darkly, 'I've always had a talent for satisfying the hungry.' He looked deep into her eyes, tracing around her features with his fingertips. He sighed.

'That night,' he said, 'after the concert, I wanted you — God I wanted you, everything . . . body and soul, just you. I didn't know what you must have thought of me — I kept telling myself that you kissed me back but I couldn't really believe it. I thought you still cared for Phillippe, that in your head it was him you were kissing, not me.'

'Oh, Max!' And I wanted you too, so very much.' She laughed at the irony of it. 'How ridiculous,' she exclaimed suddenly. 'Why didn't I just tell you.

Why didn't you tell me. I thought I was just a friend, that the kisses were for Jane.'

'Oh, my darling — the anger was mainly for her although a little was for myself, my inadequacy at handling things as I should have done — with her and with you. But the kisses were all for you; I didn't tell you because I was afraid — you opened me up, made me feel defenceless. I've failed once before.'

'You gave her too much rein?' Janet suggested.

'What an odd thing for an enlightened girl to say!'

'No — even an enlightened girl likes to know just where she stands,' she told him, grinning provocatively.

'Is that so?' he queried, his dry humour returning.

Janet gurgled, slipping a couple of fingers inside his shirt and tickling him. 'I'll go very well on a short rein,' she said, 'most fillies do.'

'Ah, no!' he said, pulling her against

him and crushing her so hard in his arms that she gasped out aloud, 'you, darling girl, won't be on any rein at all, you'll be right here.'

He began to kiss her again with an urgency that told her without any doubt how he felt about her. His hands moved across her back and down over her lips. She was enormously aware of the sheer physical strength of his body, the power and energy in his arms and thighs. In relation to her own size and strength he was immeasurably superior, yet she knew he would never use that advantage to vanquish and subdue her.

'I love you,' she murmured, revelling in the luxury of winding her fingers into his thick brown hair.

The minutes tumbled by. 'I'll never get you on board at this rate,' Max said suddenly, glancing at the clock on the dashboard.

She had her eyes closed. 'Mm — I don't want to go.'

'Oh yes you do!'

'Yes I do — but I don't want to leave you.'

'You'll soon be back — and I shall expect the very highest achievement!'

'Naturally,' she laughed.

'From my future wife,' he added, as though it were just an afterthought.

'Of course,' she said with magnificent composure considering the wild leapings that her heart was making.

'Of course,' he echoed gravely — 'so when?'

'When will I be your wife?'

'Yes.'

'Soon!'

'Very soon!'

'Oh, yes,' she hugged him, 'yes, yes, yes!'

'You won't go off and marry someone else?' he asked, outwardly jesting.

She flung herself on to him and rained kisses over his face and neck. 'Max, you know the answer to that.'

'Yes, I think I do.' He laid his forehead against hers. 'I can't wait long,' he said huskily.

'There's no need!' she reassured him. 'My contract finishes at the end of January and I shall be a free agent. My parents will be delighted to get me settled, especially my mother!'

Janet imagined her mother's face as she was introduced to Max. She felt that for her mother Max could not have been a more attractive or desirable son-in-law if she had made him up from a pattern.

'I must get you to that boat,' he said, determinedly switching on the ignition. He turned to her again, his face glowing with delighted tenderness and was unable to do anything further about starting the engine.

Eventually, with a massive surge of self-control, Janet pushed him gently away. 'They need me in Holland,' she said, smiling. 'I truly believe they need me.'

'That's good,' he said, nosing the car back on to the road. 'It's important.' He frowned a little into the mist. 'You mustn't give up your career,' he said abruptly, 'there's so much ahead for you.'

She smiled, a soft misty smile. 'Yes,' she said simply, feeling that it was important not to challenge him on this issue just at the moment.

'I mean it!' he said, his voice clipped and astringent. 'I love that independent spirit — I couldn't bear to see it go — and especially to think I was responsible.'

She gave him a playful punch. 'Of course it won't go,' she said, adding mischievously, 'and what makes you think you're going to have everything your own way?'

'Oh,' he said darkly, 'it's going to be like that is it? I should have seen the warning light when you came to my restaurant and demolished a bottle of champagne all on your own!'

'I didn't!' she gasped, 'did I?'

He turned and grinned. 'Yes,' he said, 'you did.'

'But if I hadn't,' she said slowly.

'Who knows?' he answered, taking her hand to his lips and kissing it . . .

# 11

In the springtime Janet was busy schooling a new horse for the Baron and preparing to play important parts at two weddings; bridesmaid at the first, bride at the second.

Vinnie had decided to be an Easter bride. 'He'll never have had a better Easter egg, darling,' she told Janet as they stroked the heavy oyster satin dress she had bought at Harods. 'We're going to be quite desperately happy,' she declared. 'I've made my mind up about it.'

'And you usually get what you've made your mind up about, don't you, Vinnie?' Janet asked with a twinkle in her eye.

'Of course, darling,' she said. 'That's what being female is all about.' She looked hard at her frind. 'And you're getting absolutely everything your own way at the moment, aren't you, pet?' she drawled, narrowing her eyes and running the tip of her tongue suggestively over her lips.

Janet agreed. 'I suppose I am,' she murmured.

'What a year for you, darling,' Vinnie commented.

'A second prize at an international competition, a super new horse to bring on and a fiancé who adores you so obviously he looks as though he can hardly stop himself from gobbling you up!'

'Chance would be a fine thing!' Janet laughed.

'What's the matter, pet?' Vinnie asked sharply.

'Oh,' she gave a shrug, 'I never seem to see him. I'm always working when he's free and the other way round.'

'Not a serious problem, darling?' Vinnie looked genuinely concerned.

'He's so keen for me to be independent — make my way in a career — and I just want to give some time to him. Sounds wet, doesn't it? I would never have believed it!'

'My God!' Vinnie said. 'Still, I know what you mean. I'm living in Phil's pocket at the moment and it's bliss! Being without him for too long would be like having no air to breathe!'

Vinnie certainly looked blissful on her wedding day, and some of the guests — especially the male ones — looked as though they might be short of air to breathe — her stunning auburn beauty quite took the breath away! It was a splendid affair. Janet was one of eight bridesmaids arriving at the church in a fleet of silver Rolls Corniches. The church was crowded with guests and afterwards there was lavish food and drink in a country hotel that looked as though it had once been a stately home.

The Baron, restored to good health, ate a hearty meal and gazed in affectionate contemplation at the happy couple. Janet went to talk to him when the toasts were over. 'So much beauty and talent in one couple,' he said, shaking his head. '*I* hope it will not be too great a strain for a long and happy marriage.'

'Oh dear,' Janet said, 'a sober note on a merry occasion!'

'You're allowed that at my age,' he said. 'But about you, my dear. I still worry. You're working too hard, you're not spending enough time with that nice man you're going to marry and it's showing in your eyes.'

'Oh!' she said, unable to deny anything he had said.

'Where is he my dear, anyway, I don't see him?'

'Well, it's difficult on a Saturday, and he hasn't a full staff at the moment, and . . .'

'You don't have to explain,' he said gravely. 'I understand perfectly. Just at the moment *you* need to be with him, my dear. He'll be missing you and yet he has always to be looking after his business.' His gentle eyes rested steadily on her face.

'I'm going to give you a new contract to consider,' he told her. 'Just one horse to concentrate on, no teaching and no extra horses to look after. And you will be doing it for me. Phillippe can manage on his own now. You will work only a few hours each day. I shall pay you well and when the time comes, who knows?' he raised his shoulders in an eloquent gesture, 'you can return.'

'You're not firing me then?' she asked, her eyes twinkling.

'I'm making sure that in the future my best horses have happy riders,' he said solemnly. He looked across at Phillippe, radiant at Vinnie's side. 'We both know that a horse does not give his best with a miserable, frustrated rider, do we not?'

Janet took one of the Baron's cool dry hands and kissed the palm with lingering softness. 'Thank you,' she said. 'I'm always having to thank you, aren't I?'

He patted her knee briskly. 'So — ' he said in an uncharacteristically clipped tone, 'you go back to him as soon as possible and you don't leave him for a long time. You need each other more than anything at the moment. I know all about it, my dear! You do as I say.'

★ ★ ★

The Thornlea was hushed and darkened when Janet parked Vinnie's car outside the front door.

She walked around to the side door which led directly up to Max's flat and rang the bell. Immediately a light snapped on in a window directly above. In seconds the door opened. Max, faintly ruffled and sleepy-looking, looked at his future wife and said, 'Good God! It's three o'clock in the morning?'

'Yes,' she agreed. 'I left a wonderful party, borrowed a car, drove up from London just to see you.'

'Well, you'd better come in then,' he said in his dry non-committal way. He took her into the drawing room. 'Coffee?' he asked, running a hand through his hair.

She shook her head, pulled him towards the sofa, and sat herself on his knee.

'I've come to you,' she said, 'and I'm going to stay with you.'

'Ah,' he said, eyeing her with amused alarm, 'I see.'

'You need me,' she said, 'more than the horses do or anyone or anything else for that matter.'

'Yes,' he murmured, his arms moving around her.

'Yes, yes.'

But she declined to collapse immediately into his embrace.

'And you needn't worry about my independent spirit!' she said rather fiercely.

'No?'

'No. I've never felt more independent in my whole life. I know exactly what I want and I'm determined to get it!'

He paused, then he grinned. 'I'm

convinced,' he said. 'And who am I to argue with such admirable self-assertion from such a formidably independent lady?' he asked, a faint light of mischief in his eyes.

'Max!' she exclaimed, 'I hope you're taking me seriously.'

'Oh, my darling Janet,' he murmured, 'I was never more serious in my life.'

He began to stroke her shoulders and brush his lips over her face. She pressed a kiss firmly on his mouth.

The night outside was softly dark and enfolding. His arms tightened around her.

## THE END

## CO~ 27 ~ NT HEART

### Lynne Collins

They called Romily the Snow Queen, but once she had been all fire and passion, kindled into loving by a man's kiss and sure it would last a lifetime. She still believed it would, for her. It had lasted only a few months for the man who had stormed into her heart. After Greg, how could she trust any man again? So was it likely that surgeon Jake Conway could pierce the icy armour that the lovely ward sister had wrapped about her emotions?